rothers to the Death

SAGA OF LARTEN CREPSLEY: BOOK FOUR

Other titles by

DARREN SHAN

THE SAGA OF DARREN SHAN

THE DEMONATA

THE SAGA OF LARTEN CREPSLEY

THE THIN EXECUTIONER
(one-off novel)

* Also available on audio

DARREN SHAN

Brothers to the Death

THE SAGA OF LARTEN CREPSLEY: BOOK FOUR

HarperCollins *Children's Books*

First published in hardback in Great Britain by HarperCollins *Children's Books* in 2012
This edition published in Great Britain by HarperCollins *Children's Books* in 2012
HarperCollins *Children's Books* is a division of HarperCollins*Publishers* Ltd,
77-85 Fulham Palace Road, Hammersmith, London, W6 8JB.

Visit us at
www.harpercollins.co.uk

2

978-0-00-731596-3

Printed and bound in England by Clays Ltd, St Ives plc

MIX
Paper from
responsible sources
FSC™ C007454

FSC
www.fsc.org

Find out more about HarperCollins and the environment at
www.harpercollins.co.uk/green

PART ONE

"This is what happens to lovers of vampires"

CHAPTER ONE

On a grassy bank in a park on the outskirts of Paris, a young man lay beside a middle-aged woman, holding her hand. They were talking softly, shielded from the setting evening sun by a large umbrella. Those passing by thought they were perhaps a mother and son. None suspected that the orange-haired gentleman in the blood-red suit was more than twice the age of the woman.

"What do you think people would say if I kissed you?" Larten murmured.

Alicia giggled. "There would be a scandal." Much about her had changed over the years, but her giggle was the same as ever.

"I relish a juicy scandal," Larten said, leaning closer towards her.

"Don't!" Alicia laughed, pushing him away. "You know I don't like it when you tease me."

"What if I was not teasing?" Larten asked with a

smile. But the smile was for Alicia's benefit. He was serious — he *did* want to kiss her.

"That's sweet of you," Alicia said. "But I'm an old woman. You can't have any real interest in me after all these decades. I'm a wrinkly hag!"

"Hardly," Larten snorted. Alicia looked much older than him now, but in his eyes she was as beautiful as when they'd first met almost thirty years ago.

Alicia rolled away from him, into the sunlight, where she stretched and lazily studied the clouds. Larten's smile never faltered, but inside he felt sad. It had been a decade and a half since his reunion with Alicia. They had met often over the course of those years. Each time he hoped she'd kiss him, declare her love for him, accept him as her husband. He wanted things to be like they were in 1906, when they were engaged and madly in love.

But Alicia felt that she was too old to marry again, and if she ever did give her hand to another man, she wanted to give it to a man her own age. It didn't matter that Larten had been born almost eighty years before her. He looked like he was in his twenties and that was how she thought of him. To Alicia he could never be more than a friend. Larten had accepted that – he had no choice – but he couldn't help wishing he was more.

"The children are having fun," Alicia noted, nodding at a boy and girl playing by the edge of a small pond.

The girl was almost eighteen, a young woman who would probably marry soon and have children of her own. But Larten still thought of her as little Sylva. She was a tall, slim, pretty maid, but to him she would always be a cute, chubby baby.

The *boy* was in his thirties, but didn't look much older than Sylva. He was a vampire like Larten, ageing only one year for every ten that passed. He was of medium height, but broad, built like a wrestler. He could have thrown Sylva to the far side of the pond, but he always handled her gently, as Larten had taught him, careful never to squeeze too hard when he was holding her hand, knowing he could shatter every bone in her fingers if he did.

Gavner hadn't wanted to return to Paris. He had left under a cloud, swearing loyalty to Tanish Eul, a weak, selfish vampire who had killed an innocent woman to save his own thickly-layered neck. When Larten caught up with them and herded the killer to his execution, Gavner thought his world had ended. He hated the man whom he'd known since childhood as Vur Horston, and yearned to strike him dead.

Larten had granted him that opportunity. Handing Gavner a knife, the General told him that he had killed

Gavner's parents. He said that Gavner had every right to extract revenge and he offered himself to the bewildered teenager.

Gavner would never forget how close he'd come to stabbing Larten. His mind was in a whirl. Tanish Eul's sudden death had shocked him. When he learnt that Larten had killed his parents too, it seemed like the only way to end the madness was to murder the orange-haired vampire. His fingers tightened and he tried to drive the knife forward into Larten's heart, stopping it forever.

But something held him back. He still wasn't sure why he hadn't struck. Maybe it had been the calm acceptance in Larten's eyes, the fact that he wasn't afraid of death, that he felt like he deserved to die. Perhaps it was because the vampire had been true to him for the first time in his life, and Gavner couldn't kill a man for telling the truth. Or maybe he just didn't have a killer's instinct.

Whatever the reason, Gavner had let the knife drop, collapsed in a weeping huddle and given himself over to confusion and grief.

"I wish you could spend more time with us," Alicia sighed as Gavner chased Sylva around the pond, threatening to throw her in. "Sylva misses you when you're not here."

"I suspect she misses Gavner more," Larten remarked wryly. He had never been much of a father figure. He'd always been distant with Sylva, and especially with Gavner. It was a mystery to him why the pair liked him so much.

"Gavner's like a brother to her," Alicia admitted, "but she's fond of you too. She thinks of you as an uncle."

"*Uncle Larten*," the vampire chuckled, blushing slightly. "How ridiculous."

"Don't be so stuffy," Alicia growled, pinching his left cheek until his scar burnt whitely. Then she smiled, kissed one of her fingers and pressed it to the scar. "You still haven't told me how you got that," she said, changing the subject.

"I will one night," Larten promised. "When you are old enough."

The pair laughed. Gavner heard the laughter – his senses were much sharper than a human's – and he paused to smile in the direction of the couple who had been the only real parents he'd ever known. (He tried not to think about the nights when he had served as Tanish Eul's surrogate son. While he would never speak ill of Tanish, who had been nothing but loving to Gavner, he was ashamed that he had not seen through the killer's mask.)

Larten and Vancha March had helped Gavner recover. They'd told him much about the clan, explained Tanish's bitter history, helped prepare him for life as a creature of the night. When they left Petrograd, Larten urged Gavner to travel with Vancha. He said that the Prince could teach Gavner more than he ever could. But Gavner asked to learn from Larten instead. He had always wanted to get closer to the aloof, tall man with the scar. He saw this as a chance to gain a father. There were no more lies between them. He hoped to build a strong relationship with Larten Crepsley, to earn his respect and love.

Larten did respect Gavner, and loved him in his own strange way. But he never made any open display of affection. He was shy with most people, slow to reveal anything personal. But it went beyond shyness with Gavner. He had orphaned the boy and would never allow himself to forget that. He had told Gavner the whole sad story, how he'd been suffering with a fever, how his young assistant had been killed, the way he'd lost his mind and slaughtered a shipful of humans.

Gavner had forgiven him – he had come close to killing when he lost Tanish Eul, so he could empathise with the older vampire – but Larten still blamed himself, and every time he looked at Gavner he was reminded of that dark day, of the stain on his soul. Though he had spent most of the last fifteen years with the youth, teaching him the ways of the clan, he'd always kept his assistant at arm's length, insisting Gavner treat him as nothing more than a tutor.

"I will never be a father to you," he'd declared several years ago, after Gavner had absentmindedly referred to Larten as his father. "I do not deserve such love and I will cast you aside if you ever speak of me in that way again. I will accept your friendship if you feel I am entitled to it, but no more than that."

Gavner knew that Larten thought of him as more than a mere assistant, just as he thought of Larten as more than a mentor. But he accepted the older vampire's rules and never again spoke of his true feelings. If this was what Larten needed in order to feel comfortable around his student and would-be son, so be it. He would do anything to please the man who had reluctantly reared him.

While Gavner studied Larten and Alicia, smiling sadly as he thought of the past, Sylva snuck up on him and pushed him hard. Gavner yelped, arms flailing, then fell into the water. He came up spluttering and roaring. He looked for Sylva, to drag her in, but she'd already fled — she knew how swiftly a vampire could react.

"Hide me!" Sylva squealed, seeking shelter behind her mother and Larten.

"If you were my daughter I would spank you," Larten growled as Gavner hauled himself out of the pond. "You know that sunlight is bad for him. I will have to help him fish his hat out of the pond before his hair catches fire."

Sylva's smile faded as she stared at the glowering vampire. But then Larten winked and she knew that everything was fine. She looked on with delight as he hurried to the shivering Gavner, expressing concern for him — then howled with glee as he shoved his unsuspecting assistant back into the pond.

"Men never grow up," Alicia tutted, but she was smiling too. She offered Gavner the rug she was sitting on when they returned and helped him dry his hair. She corrected him when he cursed Larten and Sylva – "Gentlemen do not use such crude words" – then packed up and led them home.

Gavner and Sylva strayed ahead of their elders, walking arm in arm. Sylva chatted about friends, fashion and movies, and Gavner pretended to be interested in such things. He had already forgiven her for pushing him into the pond — he'd never been one to hold a grudge. Larten and Alicia followed leisurely, strolling like any ordinary couple.

"How long can you stay this time?" Alicia asked, already knowing the answer. Larten and Gavner had arrived a week earlier, and though nothing had been said, she'd gathered within a few hours that it would be a short visit. Larten always tried to cram in a lot if he wasn't staying long. When she heard him making plans for all the things that he wanted to do, she knew the pair would be moving on in a matter of days, not weeks or months. By his expression this afternoon, she realised the time had come for them to leave, so she asked the question at last, the same way she always did. It was a long-established routine of theirs.

"We go tonight," Larten said. "We have a meeting which we must attend. It is not far from here as vampires measure things, but it will take us most of the night to get there."

"Will you return soon?" she asked, again already knowing the answer.

Larten sighed. "I do not think so. We have been forced to deal with unpleasant but determined people, and I suspect the negotiations will take some time."

"How mysterious your lives are," Alicia said enviously. "I bet you're off to meet a magician or witch."

"Nothing so fanciful," Larten smiled. "I would prefer it if we were. These men pose more of a threat to the world, I fear, than any being of magic."

"What do you mean?" Alicia asked, frowning at him as they reached the small house where she and Sylva lived.

"We do not have much to do with human politicians or soldiers," Larten said, pausing at the door to cast one last glance at the setting sun. "But occasionally a group tries to forge links with us and we find ourselves having to deal with them. This is one such time and I am worried about the outcome. Tell me, Alicia, what do you know about *Nazis?*"

CHAPTER TWO

"We are so alike," Franz said with a smile. "Vampires and National Socialists are creatures of similar beliefs and habits. We have common goals and hopes. If we unite, it will benefit both our *clans*." The officer's smile widened. Larten had never met people who smiled as freely as the Nazis. But he found no warmth or humour in their grins, merely menace, deceit and threats.

The Nazis had been courting the night walkers for several years. Their leader was a man who believed in the supernatural. He had set his followers the task of finding out whether or not vampires were real. The members of the clan were usually adept at keeping their secrets, but somebody had let their guard down at some point and discussed their ways with one of the investigators. It didn't happen often, but it wasn't without precedent — Larten himself had accidentally given some of their secrets away to Bram Stoker when the author was researching his book *Dracula*.

The Nazis had been politely hounding the Generals of the clan ever since they found out about them. The Princes had avoided the entreaties of the political party, as they always did whenever a group tried to forge links with them. It had happened a few times over the centuries. Vampires were faster and stronger than humans. They would make powerful allies... powerful *weapons*. The Nazis weren't the first to seek the support of the creatures of the night.

But no other group had pressed as hard as the smiling soldiers in the sharp suits. No army or party had claimed to share so many common ideals. Nobody had promised as much as the representatives of the short man with the silly-looking moustache.

Many Generals were in favour of a union with the Nazis. They saw shades of themselves in the Germans. Like vampires, National Socialists believed in honour, order, unity. They had stabilised a country in chaos. They lived by strict laws and preached obedience and decency. They had little time or sympathy for the weak or old — they focused on the strong, the pure, those who could handle themselves in a fight. They were more interested in control and power than vampires were, but apart from that they were as close to the clan in spirit as any humans had ever appeared to be.

Some highly ranked Generals had met with members

of the party in recent years, and now a Prince had been sent to parlay. Mika Ver Leth was chosen to head the debate, mostly because he was young and open to new ideas. (Though Larten thought the fact that he dressed in black and looked like a Nazi also played a part in the decision.)

This was the first time a Prince had negotiated with a human delegation and it was a momentous event in the history of the clan. Mika had to choose a General to be his second, someone he could discuss the complex issues with. Most thought he would opt for an elderly vampire with a proven record, but to everyone's surprise – not least of all Larten's – he had asked for Seba Nile's ex-student.

The pair had been engaged in talks with the Nazis for several weeks. Franz was only the latest in a line of party members that they had dealt with. They'd been treated to a tour of Germany, to meet a variety of the National Socialists in the flesh. Mika had read many documents about the party, their beliefs and aims. They had dined well, slept in fine hotels and been treated like honoured dignitaries.

Yet Larten hadn't felt at ease since linking up with Mika. He couldn't put his finger on the exact reason for his discomfort. He just didn't trust these people. They reminded him in some ways of Tanish Eul, only far more dangerous than the cynical, self-serving Tanish had ever been.

Larten listened with a polite expression but heavy heart as Franz outlined a list of reasons why vampires should support the growing Nazi movement. He promised to provide the clan with an army of new, German recruits. They would be equals, sharing all that came their way. He said the Nazis wished to learn from the wise vampires and emulate their great deeds, to turn the world away from the petty vices of the day, towards the noble pursuits of the night.

Gavner Purl and Arra Sails sat several feet behind Mika and Larten. Arra was a respected General now, but she still considered Mika to be her mentor. When he had need of her, she acted as his assistant, the way Gavner assisted Larten. She hadn't hesitated when he'd asked her to come with him. There was no dishonour in serving the wishes of a Prince, no matter how experienced a General you might be.

Larten hadn't spoken much with Arra. Their nights were packed with meetings and fact-finding outings, and by day they slept. Besides, he wasn't sure what to say. He had made his admiration of her clear in the past, but that was before he'd renewed his relationship with Alicia. His French amour might only be a close friend now, but he still hoped that she would one night ask to be more. Any romantic entanglement with Arra would have felt like a betrayal. It was easier to keep out of her way and avoid a potentially complicated situation.

"The world is changing," Franz said. He was still smiling, but not as widely as before. Larten had sensed a change in the atmosphere over the last few nights. The Nazis had grown impatient and Franz was having a hard time hiding his mounting frustration.

"The world is forever changing," Mika said.

"True," Franz nodded. "But now more than ever. Faster than ever. A storm is coming. We will all need friends if we are to survive. You will find us friends of the highest calibre. Strong. Loyal. Dependable."

"What are you like as enemies?" Mika asked casually, and although he said it with a chuckle, Larten saw Franz's face darken.

"Why speak of us that way?" Franz growled. "We have no wish to be anything but your allies."

"You misunderstand me," Mika said. "If we become your friends, your enemies will be our enemies. If you go to war, it will be *our* war. I want to know how you plan to deal with those who don't share your vision for the future."

"I see." Franz was beaming again. "First, it is important to recognise that we do not seek war. We hope to expand and re-draw the boundaries of our once-great nation, to again be a force of true power in the world. Ideally we will exert our influence peacefully. If others resist and threaten us, we will of course fight — and win — but war isn't something we wish to actively pursue."

"Yet there are some you long to destroy," Mika pressed. "People of certain nations and religions…"

"*Destroy* is the wrong word," Franz purred. "We believe this world would be better without certain types of people. We have always been upfront about that. But vampires share those beliefs. You cut loose the old and infirm, those of low character, base creatures who would drag you down. We seek to do the same. Surely that cannot be an issue for proud, pure warriors such as yourselves?"

Mika nodded slowly, considering Franz's words. This was the heart of their debate, even though they had largely skirted the issue so far. Vampires came from all corners of the earth, regardless of colour, race or creed. If you were strong, determined and honest, you could join the clan and be entitled to respect. The Nazis weren't so eager to include people of specific backgrounds.

"What do you think?" Mika asked suddenly, turning to Larten.

The orange-haired vampire blinked and stared at the Prince. Larten still wasn't sure why Mika had invited him to be his second. The raven-like Prince had said little to the General. He hadn't asked for Larten's views or discussed matters with him in detail. Until now.

As Larten struggled to form a polite, diplomatic response, Mika shook his head. "Don't tell me what you think I want to hear. And don't worry about our hosts. I want your true opinion. Share your thoughts with me, openly and honestly. That is the vampire way," he murmured to Franz and the officers who flanked him. "I hope you won't be offended."

"Of course not," Franz said, but he was squinting at Larten suspiciously.

"On which particular points do you wish me to comment, Sire?" Larten asked.

"All of them," Mika said. "I want your general reaction. Tell me what you think of the National Socialists and their desire to merge with us."

"I dislike and distrust them," Larten said bluntly. Some of the officers gasped but Franz silenced them with a sharp gesture. He was glaring at Larten, but he said nothing, waiting to hear the rest.

"They are cruel," Larten went on. He didn't enjoy airing his feelings this way, but Mika had asked him to

25

be open, and Larten would never disobey the demands of a Prince. "Vampires are hard, yes. We ask much of ourselves and those who would be part of the clan. We execute the mad, the weak, the injured, the old, or urge them to make an end of their own. In that respect we are like these humans.

"But those we treat harshly have chosen the path of the night. They left their human ways behind when they joined the clan. They understand why we treat them so pitilessly. They acknowledge our rule, live by our laws, accept death when they are no longer fit to fight.

"The enemies… no, the *victims* of the Nazis have no such choice. These people hate without reason. They pass judgement on innocents. In that way we differ. Vampires are harsh, Nazis are vicious. We are merciless, they are monstrous."

One of the officers cursed and leapt to his feet. He drew a pistol and levelled it at Larten. Before he could fire, Franz barked a command and the officer angrily holstered his weapon and sat. When he had control of the room again, Franz faced Larten and sneered. "You understand nothing of us or the problems we face."

"Perhaps," Larten said calmly. "But I was asked for my opinion and I gave it."

"Do you share his view?" Franz snapped at Mika.

The Prince smiled thinly. "In any group you will find people of differing beliefs and standards. I'm sorry if my assistant's criticism upset you. I simply wanted to know where he stood on this issue."

"And now you know," Franz said. "But where do *you* stand?"

"I will have to think about that before I give my answer." Mika rose and offered his hand. Franz hesitated, then shook the Prince's hand.

"We have been patient," the officer said softly, "but we cannot wait forever. I must know if you are with us or against us, and I need to know soon."

"You shall," Mika promised. "I'm close to making a decision. There are just a few minor matters I need to think over. You will have your answer shortly."

Franz didn't look happy, but he nodded curtly and took his seat, watching with narrowed, hostile eyes as the Prince and his followers slipped out of the room and returned to the fabulous hotel suite where they had been quartered.

CHAPTER THREE

Mika said nothing to Larten on their way back to the hotel, and retired to his room as soon as they got there, giving no indication whether or not he approved of what Larten had said. Gavner shared a worried glance with his master, then went to his own room. A distracted Larten nodded goodnight to Arra in the lobby, but as he climbed the stairs he realised she was following him. He glanced over his shoulder questioningly.

"It's time we had a chat," Arra said, then brushed ahead and waited for him at the door to his suite.

Arra cast a scornful eye around the room when she entered, unimpressed by the florid furniture and antiques. "Do you sleep in the bed?" she asked.

"Where else?" Larten replied.

"I laid hands on a coffin when I came here," she said. "I've had it shipped from one hotel to another. Beds are for humans."

Larten smiled. "You sound like Vancha March."

"A most noble vampire," Arra nodded, then sat on the least comfortable-looking chair and studied Larten seriously. She hadn't changed much since he had first met her. By no means beautiful, but pretty in her own way. She'd picked up scars in battle since she'd become a vampire, and was leaner than when she'd served as Evanna's apprentice. But she wore the same brown clothes, and in the dim light she could have passed for a teenager.

"You spoke passionately tonight," Arra noted.

"I said what was in my heart."

"The Nazis didn't like being called monsters."

Larten shrugged. "Perhaps that was uncalled for. But their smug smiles sicken me. I wished to wipe the grins from their faces."

"You certainly did that." Like Mika, Arra gave no sign whether she felt Larten had been right to speak the way he had. Before he could ask, she said, "Why don't you like me any more?"

Larten blinked. "What do you mean?"

"You craved me before. You tried to sweet talk me into taking you as a mate on many occasions. Even when you weren't openly flattering me, your gaze trailed me everywhere I went. But now you look away when I'm around. Why?"

Larten laughed. "Evanna herself could not have put the question in more direct a fashion!"

"Never mind that barmy old witch," Arra huffed. "Tell me why I repulse you."

"You do not *repulse* me," Larten said softly. "On the contrary, I think you are as striking as ever. But circumstances have changed. There is another woman…"

"You've mated?" Arra snapped.

"No. She is human."

"Then you've married?"

"No."

"You're engaged?" Arra pressed.

"Not exactly."

Arra's dark brown eyes hardened. "Are you even partners?"

Larten cleared his throat. "We were in the past, but now we are just friends."

"You wish to be more," Arra guessed, "but she won't have you."

"She thinks she is too old for me." Larten thought that Arra would laugh, but she didn't. Instead she stunned him with her next sentence.

"*I* have a mate. I mated five years ago with Darvin Allegra. You don't know him. He's a fine General, a fierce fighter, though not as passionate in the coffin as I had hoped he'd be."

"Arra!" Larten gasped. "You cannot say things like that!"

"I can if it's true," she retorted.

"What about Mika? I always thought…"

She shook her head. "I rejected his advances in the past, and I doubt if he will ever choose a mate now. He has no time for love these nights. He takes his duties as a Prince very seriously."

"Why did Darvin not come here with you?" Larten asked.

"He wasn't invited," Arra said. "Business is business. Besides, he knows I plan to take you as a mate in the future and he's jealous. I don't think he—"

"Stop!" Larten roared, blushing furiously. "How can you say such things when you already have a partner?"

"I'll be free in two years," Arra said. "It was a seven-year agreement and I have no intention of signing up for another spell. I'll be faithful to Darvin for the next twenty-four months, but after that…"

Larten gawped at the dark-haired vampiress. "You were never this frank in the past," he mumbled. "You teased me and kept me at arm's length."

"That's what young women do to their admirers," Arra sniffed. "But I'm older. I'm not interested in games now. We would be good together, so it's time we stopped fooling around."

"Do I have any say in the matter?" Larten growled.

"Not much," Arra said.

Larten could do nothing but laugh. When he'd finished chuckling, he sat close to Arra and took her hand. Her nails were sharp and jagged, and he was reminded of Evanna's nails when she'd scarred his face. He thought he might get scarred again tonight, but he didn't shy away from Arra as he spoke.

"I am fond of you, and once I was much more than fond. But I will not divide my loyalties. I love Alicia — the woman of whom I spoke — and I can think of no other while she has my heart."

"Have you been reading poetry?" Arra frowned.

"I never learnt to read," Larten said.

"But others have read poems to you?"

"On occasion," he admitted.

"Damn poets," Arra snarled. "They complicate everything." She squinted at the orange-haired vampire. "How old is your woman?"

"It would not be polite to state her age," Larten murmured.

"Is she in good health?" Arra asked. "Does she have twenty years left? Thirty? I don't mind waiting a few decades until she dies, but if it's more than that I might get restless."

"Be careful," Larten growled. "I will not have you speak so lightly of such grave matters."

"Nonsense," Arra huffed. "Humans lead short lives. That's the way it is. Don't tell me you plan to mourn for the next few centuries after she dies and remain true to her memory?"

Larten reared back and prepared a stinging insult. But before he could deliver it, somebody knocked on his door. As he stood, glaring at Arra, the door opened and Mika Ver Leth entered.

"Am I interrupting?" the Prince asked, sensing tension in the air.

Larten almost told Mika that he was, but then he smiled tightly. "No, Sire. Arra was just leaving."

"No, stay," Mika said as Arra rose. "You should hear this too." He closed the door and stepped closer to Larten. His expression was as guarded as ever. "You said a lot with few words tonight."

"I spoke honestly, Sire, as you bid," Larten responded.

Mika nodded. "I was aware of your dislike of our German suitors – you haven't learnt to hide your emotions as artfully as I have – but I didn't know you felt so strongly about them. Do you stand by everything that you said?"

"Aye," Larten said evenly.

"Good," Mika grunted. "The Nazis disgust me. I'm

pleased you feel the same way. They're creatures of destruction and hatred. I had to be diplomatic and give them every opportunity to present their case. But I've been drawing closer to my decision all the time, and tonight settled matters for me.

"I'm sorry I asked you to speak your mind in front of such vile animals," Mika went on, "but I needed to bait them, to give them one last chance to deny such foul accusations. If they weren't monsters, they would have argued when you criticised them. But since they are, they could only threaten violence. I couldn't be the one to enrage them, so I used you. Again, my apologies."

Larten smiled. "You have nothing to apologise for, Sire. It was a pleasure to tell them what I thought. If I had known of your intentions, I would have treated them to even more of my mind."

"No, that was enough," Mika said. Then he sighed. "Franz was truthful about one thing — a storm *is* coming. But it's a storm of their making. Humanity is in for a rough ride, I fear. They are heading towards another *Great* War, and this one could be even worse than the last.

"We must play no part in the atrocities. We cannot even afford to observe, in case the Nazis capture and manipulate us into doing their bidding."

"No human can catch a vampire," Arra snorted.

"These might," Mika disagreed. "They're cunning. It will be best if we don't give them the chance. I'm leaving tonight to spread the word — I want every vampire out of Europe. If some are determined to stay, I'll urge them to keep deeper to the shadows than ever. We probably have a few years before war erupts, but the sooner we slip free of this spreading net of fascism, the better.

"I need you and Gavner to distract them," he said to Larten. "When you meet with Franz tomorrow, tell him I've left to discuss the matter with the other Princes. Make it seem as if you think I'm angry with you, that I plan to pledge our forces to the Nazi cause. String him along. When he realises he's been played for a fool, flee. Take to the hills, but don't flit. Let them track you. I think the Nazis will trail you in the hope that you'll lead them to Vampire Mountain. Keep that hope alive for as long as you can. Stretch it out for months... years if possible. The longer they focus their attention on you and Gavner, the more time the rest of us will have to evacuate."

"We will lead them on the mother of all wild goose chases," Larten promised, eyes alight. He would drag them through the harshest, most uncomfortable corners of the world. He doubted that Franz would smile so much then!

Mika clasped Larten's shoulder and squeezed. "Stay alert," he warned. "These men are dangerous. They might try to trap you if they suspect that they're being led astray. If that happens and they block all avenues of escape, you'll better serve the clan dead than alive. Understand?"

"We will do whatever we have to," Larten said steadily.

"I trust you completely," Mika said, "but Gavner is young. Maybe I should send Arra with you instead."

"No!" Larten yelped. When Mika looked at him strangely, Larten forced a weak chuckle. "I have faith in Gavner Purl. This will be a good test for him. If I think that he is struggling, I will send him back to Vampire Mountain. But I believe he will prove himself."

"Very well," Mika said and covered his face with his right hand, placing the tip of his middle finger to his forehead and spreading the adjoining fingers. "Even in death may you be triumphant."

Mika departed. Arra followed, but paused at the door and glanced back with a veiled smile. "This isn't over," she purred. "We'll discuss our relationship in more depth later."

Before Larten could protest, she slipped out, leaving

him alone in the large, ornate suite, to marvel at the fact that he was more worried by Arra than he was by the army of Nazis which would soon be hot on his and Gavner's trail.

CHAPTER FOUR

Larten was ready to strangle Gavner. He had endured more than three months of his assistant's snoring and it was driving him mad. He'd tried herbal medicines, pegs on Gavner's nose, even a gag, but nothing worked. He rarely got more than a couple of hours' sleep most days. He was tired and irritated, and he blamed it all on Gavner Purl.

"What's wrong with you?" Gavner yawned, sitting up and stretching. They had spent another day in a coffin in a crypt. Gavner had enjoyed a perfect day's sleep, but Larten had been up for the past hour and looked as sour as a pinched baby.

"Three guesses," Larten snapped, shooting Gavner a dark look.

Gavner laughed. "Don't tell me I was snoring again."

"I think you do it just to annoy me," Larten growled.

"You should move to another coffin if it's that bad."

Larten's expression darkened and he muttered foul

curses beneath his breath. It had been his idea to share a coffin. They holed up in graveyards most days, although sometimes they slept in barns or old ruins. They could easily have slept apart, but Larten thought it would be safer if they stayed together. He worried that the Nazis might divide and capture one of them otherwise.

The Germans had been pursuing them for the past three months, ever since Franz realised Mika wasn't returning. Negotiations had broken down and the officer was replaced by one who never smiled and who demanded Larten agree to his terms immediately — or else. Sensing that he had pushed them as far as he could, Larten stole away that night and he and Gavner had been on the run since.

Larten was enjoying the game of cat and mouse. He and Gavner kept one step ahead of the Nazis, moving swiftly every night, but never so fast that they couldn't be tracked. The Nazis had almost trapped them a few times, surrounded graveyards where they were sleeping and moved in for the kill. If Larten had been human, he and Gavner would have been caught, but his sharp sense of hearing had alerted him to the threat each time and they'd managed to break free.

On one occasion the Nazis outsmarted them and sent their forces ahead of the vampires to stake out a number of graveyards in advance. That had almost been the end — they'd faced a desperate dash at dawn to find somewhere safe to rest, ending up beneath the roots of an ancient tree. Ants and other insects had made it a long, uncomfortable day. Since then Larten had varied their route, following no set pattern, deciding each day at dusk which direction to take.

Larten wasn't sure how long the Nazis would dog their trail. Mika thought they would hound him for years. Larten doubted they were patient enough to follow him for that long, but so far they'd shown no sign of quitting. They had doubled their numbers, then doubled them again, even following the pair when they crossed the border into lands where Germans were far from welcome. Larten could have revealed the Nazis' presence to the local authorities, but his task was to lead them on, not have them locked up.

The only real downside was Gavner's snoring. It truly was as bad as Larten claimed. Some days he made more noise than one of the polar bears which Larten had wrestled with years earlier during their trek across the plains of Greenland.

"Perhaps if I cut off your nose…" Larten muttered, only half-joking.

"You go anywhere near my nose and I'll slice off your ears," Gavner retorted.

"You were not this bad when you were a child."

"How do you know? You never checked on me when I was asleep."

"Yes I did," Larten protested.

"Don't lie," Gavner tutted. "Alicia always tucked me in and looked after me if I stirred in the night. She told me I was a terrible snorer from the start."

"Then you admit it!" Larten pounced.

"Maybe I snore a *little*," Gavner grinned.

The younger vampire moved to the mouth of the crypt and stared at the rows of headstones and crosses. It was almost dusk, but the light still hurt his eyes and he had to shield them with a hand.

"How come you don't mind the sun so much?" he asked Larten.

"Your eyes adjust after fifty or sixty years," Larten told him.

Gavner grimaced. "I hate the way you make the decades sound so casual. Fifty years is a long time."

"I thought so too once," Larten said, although honestly he couldn't remember when fifty years had seemed like an age. Like most vampires who had been around for more than a century, he had the impression that he'd always been off-hand about the passage of time. He had forgotten the impatience of his youth, the way years had dragged. He no longer regarded the future with unease, wondering how he'd fill so many long nights. As a General of good standing, he had more things to worry about than killing time.

"You must get bored," Gavner said. "There must be nights when you feel like you've been alive forever, and the thought of enduring more drives you insane."

Larten cocked an eyebrow at Gavner. "You sound like a Cub. Perhaps you need to spend some time with vampires your own age."

"That lot of losers?" Gavner snorted. "No chance!"

They had run into a pack of Cubs several years earlier. There weren't as many as there had been in Larten's youth. Vampires only rarely blooded children now, and new recruits were given more time to adjust to the ways of the clan before being asked to commit themselves. As a result, few felt as restless as Larten once had. Most were not inclined to break away from the clan for a decade or two.

But some young vampires still gathered in different parts of the globe every so often, to mix with humans and lead a free and easy life before giving themselves over completely to the vampire cause. When Gavner had been introduced to a pack, he reacted with scorn. The high-living, dandyish members reminded him of Tanish Eul and he felt nothing but contempt for them. His response delighted Larten, although he did feel a pang of shame when he considered how low an opinion Gavner would have had of *him* if they had met back when he went by the name of Quicksilver.

"Are there any exercises I can do to make my eyes stronger?" Gavner asked.

"Try focusing on far-off objects," Larten said. "Fix on something in the distance and hold on it with your eyes almost shut. Slowly widen them. When the pain goes away, take a break, then focus on something else and repeat."

"That will help?" Gavner asked dubiously.

"You will start to notice a difference fairly soon," Larten said.

"How soon exactly?"

"Ten or fifteen years," Larten said with a straight face.

Gavner glared, not sure if the older vampire was joking or not. Muttering to himself – much as Larten had moments earlier – he settled against the wall of the crypt near the door and commenced the exercise. Hiding a smile, Larten set about preparing their first meal of the night. He cooked a couple of rabbits which Gavner had caught earlier, using collapsible pans which Evanna had given him.

"Any rumblings from the Nazis during the day?" Gavner asked after a while.

"How could I hear anything over the sound of your snoring?" Larten replied.

"Stuffy old bat," Gavner grunted. "You should loosen up and pull your head out of your..." He stopped. Larten thought it was because he didn't want to complete the insult, but seconds later Gavner said, "Someone's there."

"Where?" Larten darted to Gavner's side.

Gavner pointed. "On the outskirts of the graveyard. Under that tree. I can't see anyone now, but there was a man a moment ago."

"A Nazi?" Larten asked.

"I don't think so. He was small, white hair, dressed in yellow."

"With green boots?" Larten said quickly.

"Yes. You know him?"

"Aye." Larten's face was dark.

"Is he a vampire?"

Larten shook his head. "If your eyes were sharper, you would have seen a heart-shaped watch sticking out of his breast pocket."

Gavner drew a sharp breath. "Mr Tiny?"

"I suspect so."

Larten had told Gavner much about the mysterious meddler, the man of ancient years who claimed to be an agent of destiny. For a long time he had said nothing of their meeting in Greenland, when Desmond Tiny pulled him back from the brink of a deadly fall, sparing both their lives for dark, unknowable reasons of his own. But finally, since Gavner kept asking, he told the full story even though it troubled the young vampire.

"Why is he here?" Gavner asked, searching with his gaze for the strange, short man. "Doesn't he only turn up when terrible things are about to happen?"

"He is never far from disaster," Larten said, "but he sometimes pays visits for other reasons." He hesitated, then decided this was as good an occasion as any to tell Gavner another of his secrets. "This is not the first time he has trailed us."

Gavner looked around, his eyes narrowing, but not from the sunlight.

"I have caught glimpses of him several times over the decades," Larten said. "He circles us occasionally, keeping his distance, watching."

"Why?" Gavner snapped.

Larten shrugged.

"Maybe we should go after him," Gavner suggested. "Face up to him. Make him explain why he follows us."

"There is no point," Larten sighed. "He never comes close enough to catch. The nearest he came to me was when I visited my old home last year."

45

Larten had been back to the city of his birth a few times with Gavner. He liked to keep an eye on the place. Relatives of his still lived there, and although he had not tracked down any of them, he felt connected. Whenever he was within easy travelling distance, he made time to swing by and make sure that all was well with the people who had been his before he was accepted into the clan.

"I was on the roof of the house where my parents used to live," Larten went on. "You were asleep — snoring, it goes without saying. Mr Tiny appeared on the roof next to mine. I thought he was going to say something – he stood there for ages, looking at me directly – but then he turned and left."

"Why didn't you tell me?" Gavner asked.

"I saw no reason to trouble you."

Gavner scowled. "I'm not a child. I don't need to be protected."

"It had nothing to do with protection," Larten said. "I simply did not wish to burden you with information which would have been of no use to you."

"How do you know it wouldn't have been useful?" Gavner grumbled. "I could have watched out for him. I might have been able to trap him."

"No one can trap Desmond Tiny," Larten said. "When he does not want to be approached, it is impossible to get close to him. While he obviously finds the pair of us fascinating for some reason, it is equally clear that he has no interest in speaking with us. We would only waste our time if we—"

"That's where you're wrong," somebody said brightly, and both vampires reeled away from the entrance to the crypt.

As they recovered, they saw someone squatting outside the mouth of their den. He was blocking most of the light, but as he ducked forward, their eyes focused on a chubby, rosy, beaming face.

"Well," Mr Tiny chuckled, rocking back and forth on his heels, shattering a small bone underfoot as he did so, "isn't anyone going to invite me in?"

CHAPTER FIVE

Larten offered Mr Tiny one of the rabbits, but he turned it down. "I prefer my meat raw," he said scoldingly. "Where's the pleasure in eating if you can't feel the juices streaming down your chin as you bite in?"

The short man was perched on one of the coffins. He had kicked off his left boot and was scratching the flesh of his foot with a bone he'd picked up from the ground. Larten was intrigued to see that Mr Tiny's toes were webbed.

"You've grown a lot since our paths first crossed," Mr Tiny said to Gavner.

"That was a long time ago," Gavner said softly.

"Hardly," Mr Tiny snorted, then eyed Gavner critically. "You were an ugly baby. At least that much hasn't changed."

Gavner bristled, but Mr Tiny only laughed and turned his attention to Larten. "I assume you're aware of the dozens of stout-hearted Germans dogging your every move?"

"Yes," Larten said.

Mr Tiny flicked the bone he'd been scratching his foot with up into the air. He let it spin a couple of times, then caught it and proceeded to pick his teeth with it. Larten raised an eyebrow, but said nothing. There was a long silence. Gavner felt uneasy, but Larten and Mr Tiny both looked at ease.

Mr Tiny broke the silence. "You've matured since I saved you in that palace of ice. You remind me of Seba Nile now, serious and boring."

"I am not a jester," Larten said calmly. "It is not my job to amuse you."

Mr Tiny scowled. "I preferred you when you were suicidal." He cast a cat-like glance at Gavner. "Has he told you about the time he nearly leapt to his death?"

"Yes," Gavner said.

Mr Tiny rolled his eyes. "You two are about as much fun as…" He grumbled his way into silence again.

Larten cleared his throat. "Have you travelled far?"

"I'm always travelling," Mr Tiny replied. "I never stop in one place for long. There's always some new tragedy to enjoy, a fresh disaster which merits an audience. I don't get home often."

"You have a home?" Gavner asked.

"Of course," Mr Tiny said. "Every man needs a place to put his feet up and call his castle. I might take you there one day, Master Purl. You could tell me tall tales and admire my collection."

"What do you collect?" Gavner asked, but Mr Tiny waved the question away and cocked his head. "Ah. Here they come. Better late than never."

Larten and Gavner shared an uncertain look. They couldn't hear anything. Then, out of nowhere, Larten heard the footsteps of several heavy people, close to the entrance to the crypt. He couldn't understand how they had got so near without alerting him before this. It was as if they had dropped to the earth or appeared out of thin air.

As Larten tensed and Gavner rose to his feet, eight strange figures entered the crypt and fanned out around Mr Tiny's coffin. They were even shorter than the meddler in yellow, and all were dressed in blue robes with hoods drawn over their heads to hide their faces.

"The Little People," Larten sighed, having heard the legends.

"I must come up with a better name for them one day," Mr Tiny purred, leaning across to adjust the hood of the Little Person closest him. Larten caught a glimpse of grey skin which had been stitched together, and a flash of green which might have been the creature's eyes. Its mouth was covered with some sort of mask. Before he could probe further, the hood fell back into place and he saw nothing more of the Little Person's face.

"I'm taking them to the Cirque Du Freak," Mr Tiny said, and Larten's eyes lit up.

"The Cirque is nearby?" he gasped, surprising Gavner with his enthusiasm.

Mr Tiny nodded. "Just a few hours from here. That's why I'm in the area. You didn't think I dropped by just to pass the time with you and your pup, did you?"

"Don't call me a—" Gavner growled, taking a menacing step forward. Before he got any further, four of the Little People stepped in front of him and shielded Mr Tiny. They made no sounds and he couldn't see their faces, but Gavner got the impression that they were snarling hungrily beneath their hoods.

"If you don't withdraw, they'll tear you limb from limb and eat your flesh while it's warm and bloody," Mr Tiny said cheerfully. He studied Gavner speculatively. "I believe I'll ask them to keep your tongue for me."

Gavner retreated swiftly, only stopping when he backed into the wall. The Little People returned to their original positions. Mr Tiny looked disappointed.

Larten had taken no notice of the exchange. He was searching mentally for Mr Tall, the owner of the

Cirque Du Freak. The pair had bonded years before and Larten could track him the same way he could track Seba and Wester.

After a few seconds the orange-haired vampire smiled. Mr Tiny had told the truth — his old friend was no more than a couple of hours away. Larten brightened at the thought of meeting with Mr Tall again. He adored the world of the Cirque Du Freak, its fantastical performers, the magical shows it produced without fail night after night.

"You can come with me," Mr Tiny said. "I won't be stopping — I just want to drop off my Little People — but you can stay once I'm gone."

Larten would have loved to accept the tiny man's offer, but as he thought about it, his excitement dwindled. He didn't want to lead the Nazis to the Cirque Du Freak — it might mean complications for Mr Tall and his crew. Better to steer clear and return at a later date when he was free of his vampiric duties.

"No, thank you," Larten said. "We must move on. We do not have time for social visits."

"As you like," Mr Tiny sniffed. He got to his feet, put his boot back on and started for the exit.

"One moment," Larten stopped him.

"Yes?" Mr Tiny paused.

"If you do not mind my asking, could you tell me why you are taking the Little People to the Cirque Du Freak?"

Mr Tiny shrugged. "I have a vested interest in the Cirque. Hibernius Tall might be my polar opposite when it comes to height, but we share many similar concerns. I help out in times of distress. Hibernius can usually take care of himself, but he doesn't always act in his own best interest. Sometimes he is powerless to shield his performers from the cruelties of the world. In times of danger and terrible wars, I send a troop of Little People to travel with the Cirque and guard the cast and crew from catastrophe."

"But this is not a time of war," Larten noted.

"It will be soon," Mr Tiny chuckled, his eyes flashing with wicked delight. "The most delicious war ever will be hot upon us within a matter of years. I can't wait. It's going to be majestic. I plan to follow it in all its gory glory, so I need to see to Hibernius in advance, to avoid getting distracted later."

"You cannot know that for certain," Larten said. "Like you, I think there will be another savage war, but it is a guess. Neither of us can be sure."

"*I* can," Mr Tiny purred. "Time is not the mystery for me that it is for you. I can see into the future. I know what lies ahead."

"If that is true, you could stop it," Larten said. "You could intervene and halt it at its source."

"I could," Mr Tiny said thoughtfully, then grinned viciously. "But that wouldn't be any fun!"

Mr Tiny threw a mock salute at Larten and Gavner then ducked out of the crypt. His Little People followed like a line of giant, gloomy ducks. Larten and Gavner stared at each other. Before they could say anything, Mr Tiny stuck his head back inside. "I almost forgot — you'll be seeing your old friend Wester Flack soon. Give him my regards, won't you?"

"Wester?" Larten snapped. "What is he doing here and how do you...?"

Before he could complete the question, Mr Tiny was gone, leaving a troubled Larten and a bewildered Gavner alone in the crypt with the remains of the dead.

CHAPTER SIX

A week later, with the Nazis hot on their trail, Wester caught up with Larten and Gavner on a wind-swept mountain. It was raining heavily. The pair had been searching for a cave where they could rest during the day. Larten spotted Wester from a long way off, but they kept searching while the guard closed in on them.

Larten hugged Wester when he arrived. The pair were like brothers and had been for most of their lives.

"It is a joy to see you," Larten greeted him.

"You too," Wester smiled, but he looked drawn and tired. He started to speak, but Larten shook his head and wiped rain from his face.

"Help us find a cave. We can talk when we are sheltered and dry."

Wester scoured the mountain with the others. In the end they found a tiny cave – little more than a hole – and squeezed into it. At least the rain wouldn't drench them here. There was no room to light a fire, but they generated enough body heat to warm the cramped space.

As they wrung the worst of the rain out of their clothes, Larten asked casually, "Why have you been consulting with Desmond Tiny?"

Wester stared at Larten, astonished. "How do you know that?"

"He paid us a visit recently."

Wester looked worried. "What did he say about me?"

"Only that you would be joining us soon. He asked me to give you his regards."

Wester scowled. "Damn his *regards*! He shocked the life out of me a couple of years ago. I was scouting around the base of Vampire Mountain – Seba had asked me to bring him some berries – and Mr Tiny hailed me from a tree."

"Desmond Tiny has returned to Vampire Mountain?" Larten snapped.

"No. He didn't enter. He said that he just happened to be passing, but I think he specifically came to see me."

Larten frowned. "Did he say why?"

Wester sighed. There were dark rims around his eyes and the flesh of his cheeks was tight. He looked like he hadn't slept much or eaten properly in a long time. "I'm losing support," he said softly. "Those who stood by me in my campaign to alert the clan to the threat of the vampaneze are trickling away. The tide of opinion is turning. Many vampires see shades of our hatred for the vampaneze mirrored in the hatred of the Nazis for their enemies. They have begun to question our motives and goals."

Wester despised the purple-skinned vampaneze. One of them had killed his family. His thirst for revenge had never ebbed. He'd linked up with others of his mindset and they had been trying to gather enough support to drive the vampires to war with their blood cousins. Larten was pleased to hear that they were losing momentum.

"Mr Tiny told me this would happen," Wester went on. "He said he can see into the future, and that within a handful of years the anti-vampaneze movement will be a wreck. All but the most passionate will desert us and war with the vampaneze will never come to pass."

"That's a good thing, isn't it?" Gavner asked innocently.

"It is if you're a vampaneze," Wester spat.

Gavner blinked. He'd met Wester a couple of times, but had never seen this side of the guard. He glanced questioningly at Larten, but the General was focused on his drained-looking friend.

"Mr Tiny thrives on war," Larten said softly. "He loves chaos, battle, death. Did he visit you in order to encourage you, to advise you on how you could rally the troops and relight the fires of hatred in the hearts of the clan?"

Wester nodded glumly. "He said *you* were the key."

Larten's features darkened. "I have never been one of your supporters. You know I do not agree with you on this point. How can I have any connection to your fortune in this regard?"

"We need a figurehead," Wester said. "I thought Arrow could be our leader, but although he hates the vampaneze as much as I do, he doesn't favour going to war. Several of our older, respected members have died in recent times, which has further weakened our cause. But they were never going to be strong enough to drive us forward. We need a youthful, talismanic figure. A Prince, ideally, or a General of high standing."

"No Prince will back you," Larten said.

"None of the current batch," Wester agreed.

Larten's eyes narrowed. "But you think you have found a future Prince who you can manipulate?"

"Not manipulate," Wester said quickly. "I'm not looking to trick anyone into doing anything they don't want to. But if I could persuade... reason with..." He trailed off and stared at the floor. "Mr Tiny said that you would become a Prince."

"Nonsense," Larten barked. "He was toying with you. He lied."

"I don't think so." Wester looked up again. "You're widely respected. Your reputation has been growing steadily since you returned from Greenland, having found the burial palace of Perta Vin-Grahl. Generals talk of you when they gather and debate your movements and deeds. Your recent criticism of the Nazis won you even more admirers. You put the feelings of the clan into a few clear, simple words. They liked that. Many who were initially in favour of a union with the Nazis changed their minds because of what *you* said."

Larten stared at his blood-brother, worried by what he was hearing. He'd never seriously thought that he might be asked to become a Prince. He knew that he had earned the respect of many in the clan, but he'd no idea feelings ran this deeply. In his own eyes he was seriously flawed. He had made a lot of mistakes, some of which he bitterly regretted. He was astonished to hear that others regarded him so highly.

"I have never sought nomination," Larten muttered. "Unlike Mika, I have no wish to become a Prince. It has never been my intention to impress."

Wester chuckled. "That's why they like you. Most Princes don't want to be leaders. They're chosen partly because of their lack of ambition, not because they desire power. Mika's an exception, but you're like the majority, a steadfast, pure-hearted, uncomplicated vampire. Generals prefer your sort."

Larten shook his head with wonder, then shrugged. "I do not know if what you say is true or an exaggeration. Either way, it makes no difference. I will go about my business as I always have. I am not concerned with the politics of Vampire Mountain. If I am ever asked to lead, I shall accept with humility and honour. If not, I will serve no less fervently.

"But if they do ask… if I do become a Prince…" His face was hard. "What good would that be to *you*?"

Wester gulped and looked aside, unable to meet his best friend's gaze. "I've never asked anything of you," he croaked, cheeks flushing. "In the matter of the vampaneze, I left you to your conscience. I would have cherished your support, but I never sought it. I asked for no favours."

"And I respect you for that," Larten said, hoping that Wester would stop there. But the slender guard couldn't.

"I need you to back me now." Larten could see how much Wester hated having to beg, but he was desperate.

That desperation struck Larten hard and he said nothing as Wester continued. "Without you, I'm lost. All the years I've devoted to this... the arguments, the winning of influential friends, the sacrifices... it will have all been for nothing. I've always believed the clan would rally and take the fight to the craven, purple traitors before they came looking for us. That belief keeps me going and defines who I am. Without it I'm nobody, a nothing."

Wester's eyes were brimming with tears and he had to pause. Larten wanted to say something, but he could think of nothing that would be of any help.

"I'm finding it hard to sustain that belief," Wester sobbed. "Friends and allies are deserting the movement. Generals scowl when I speak ill of the vampaneze. I've been told to guard my tongue, that this isn't the time for such sentiments. We were so close – closer than you can imagine – to winning over the clan. Now our dreams are unravelling. A golden opportunity is passing us by, and in a few more years the chance to strike will have been lost."

"That is for the best," Larten said. "If the clan does not desire war, why push for one?"

"Because it's going to come whether we want it or not!" Wester shouted. "The vampaneze have been promised ultimate victory over us. They're simply waiting for their fabled Lord to arise. Once he does, all will be lost. Our only chance is to stamp them out *now*, before the prediction of Mr Tiny's comes to pass."

"Mr Tiny..." Larten growled. "Have you not thought that this might be part of his plan? He predicted war between the clans, but there has been no sign that either side yearns for battle. Maybe he is using you to start the war that he longs for. The vampaneze hate the idea of leadership. They believe in true equality, no Generals or Princes. If we threaten them, perhaps their opinion will change, and maybe *that* will lead to the emergence of the Lord of the Vampaneze whom you so fear."

"Even if it does, he'll only be a Lord of corpses," Wester sneered. "If we act swiftly and brutally, we can kill them all. It will be an ugly war. Our losses will be severe. But if we can secure the future of the clan, won't it be worthwhile?"

Larten sighed. "I can never agree with you on this. We view the issue from opposing sides. Do not ask me to meet you in the middle, for on this there is no point at which we can find common ground."

"But you can change sides," Wester pressed. "If I could only convince you that you're wrong..."

"You cannot," Larten said.

"You won't even let me try?" Wester cried.

"No." Larten was firm.

Wester started to spit a retort. Then he caught himself and grimaced. "So be it," he said hoarsely. "I won't threaten our friendship over this. It's important to me, but nothing matters more than our relationship. You're my brother and I won't risk driving a wedge between us."

"Those are the wisest words I ever heard pass between your lips," Larten said, smiling with relief.

Wester laughed sickly and cocked an eyebrow. "I'll accept your position, but you're wrong, you know. We *should* go to war with the vampaneze. Time will prove me right."

"Perhaps it will," Larten said. "But for now, let us have no more talk of dark matters. Rustle us up some food, Gavner, the finest game you can find."

"On a mountain like this?" Gavner groaned. "In such foul weather?"

"A first-rate assistant always provides for his master," Larten said stiffly.

"But only a second-rate master sends his assistant out to hunt in the rain," Gavner grumbled. Nevertheless he shuffled towards the mouth of the tiny cave to do Larten's bidding.

"Don't bother," Wester stopped him. "I can't stay."

Larten made a rumbling noise. "I hope you are not leaving because of what I said."

"No." Wester smiled wryly. "I guessed you would respond negatively. I asked out of hope, not expectation. I have business elsewhere and I've come far out of my way. I will have to flit to make up time."

"It is odd that you detoured if you had a pressing appointment," Larten noted. "Why the rush to speak with me if you did not expect a positive response?"

"You're getting sharper with age," Wester chuckled, then all of the humour drained from him. "Does Alicia still live in Paris?"

Larten felt his insides tighten. He had a good nose for danger, having had so much experience of it over the centuries, and he caught a strong whiff of it now.

"Yes," Gavner answered when Larten was silent.

"The same place as when I last visited the city with you?" Wester pressed.

"No," Larten said softly. "She has moved a couple of times since then."

"Good," Wester sniffed. "This might have nothing at all to do with her – I hope that it hasn't – but I heard a rumour and felt it was vital that I inform you. That's why I came, even though time was against me." He looked around and dropped his voice, as if afraid of being overheard. "Randel Chayne has been making enquiries about you."

"I've heard that name before…" Gavner said, trying to remember where.

"He is the vampaneze who tormented Tanish Eul," Larten said. "The one who killed people who were close to Tanish."

Gavner's breath caught in his throat. "Why is he asking about *you*?"

Larten shook his head uncertainly. "I have had no dealings with Randel since that night in Paris when Tanish blamed his murders on me. I have not even thought about him. The two of us had no quarrel with one another. It was Tanish he hated, not me."

"From what I hear, Randel Chayne hates all vampires," Wester said morosely. "But he had a special spot in his heart for Tanish, and if the rumour is true, he might have transferred his attention to you."

"Tanish did not have any close friends in Paris until I came along," Larten said, thinking aloud. "That is why Randel focused on business associates of his. But maybe he has decided to hurt me in order to punish Tanish — no one outside our small circle knows that Tanish is dead. Randel would find it hard to pinpoint my location, but if he knows about Alicia…"

"How could he?" Gavner snapped.

"It is no great secret," Larten said. "We were open friends with Tanish when I lived in Paris. If Randel Chayne has been making enquiries about me, he will surely have heard of Alicia. If he also learns that I have been making trips to the city in recent years, he might correctly assume that I have been visiting Alicia and target her in the hope of discovering my whereabouts."

"I'd have gone to warn her if I could," Wester said, "but I didn't know where she was living. Even if I knew, she's never met me, so she would have had no reason to trust me. I thought it was better to bring the matter to you."

"You did right," Larten said. "We will return to Paris as soon as we can. Ideally I would like to flit, but as that is not possible, we must—"

"What are you talking about?" Gavner interrupted. "Of course you'll flit. Her life might be in danger. Sylva's too. I can't flit yet, so you'll have to go ahead of me."

Larten shook his head. "We must continue to lead the Nazis astray."

"To hell with the Nazis!" Gavner shouted. "I'll take care of them. You have to warn Alicia and Sylva."

"I cannot," Larten snarled. "I am on a mission of

vital importance to the clan. You are my assistant. I cannot leave such an important task in your hands."

"Don't tell me you're going to put your duty before Alicia and Sylva's safety," Gavner roared. He tried to square up to Larten, but the hole was too tight for him to do so.

"He must," Wester said softly, laying a hand on Gavner's broad shoulder. "I have to put my duties first too. We are tied by the vows we take when we pledge ourselves to the clan. You'll come to understand that when you spend more time among us."

Gavner stared at the vampires with disbelief. Then his face hardened. "And if Randel Chayne gets to them before we do?" he asked.

"Then I will loathe myself for the rest of my life," Larten answered coolly. "But we are not human. We put the needs of the clan before all else. It took me a long time to accept that, but now I do. We surrender many liberties when we become Generals, but without that core allegiance our clan would be a tribe of Tanish Euls.

"We will get as much rest as we can," Larten said. "When it is safe to leave, we will start for Paris. We will move swiftly, but let the Nazis stay in touch with us. We are not that far from the city. We can be there within a fortnight. Less if we are lucky."

"That's a long time to leave Alicia and Sylva unprotected," Gavner muttered.

"We will send a telegram on our way," Larten said, "telling them to move out of Paris and hide. With the luck of the vampires, that will be enough."

"And if luck isn't with us?" Gavner asked, but Larten ignored the question.

Wester and Larten clasped hands briefly, then Wester left without any words of farewell — there was nothing he could say to put Larten at his ease. The guard ran down the mountain and disappeared when he hit flitting speed. Larten wasn't watching when Wester vanished. He had already curled up into a ball and shut his eyes. If he felt guilty or scared, he kept his emotions hidden from the distraught Gavner Purl. A General of good standing was never supposed to betray what he felt inside.

CHAPTER SEVEN

The pair of vampires crossed Europe quickly, pushing the pace as much as they dared. Although Larten never gave Gavner any hint that he was thinking such things, he longed to give the Nazis the slip. He wanted to flit, ignore his promise to Mika, make sure Alicia and Sylva were safe. He thought about stealing away and leaving Gavner to deal with the Nazis by himself. He could be back in two or three nights and the Germans might never even be aware of his absence.

But if his plan backfired and they captured Gavner...

Larten trusted his assistant, but Gavner was young and inexperienced. The General had to stay with him, not only because of his duty to the clan, but because of Alicia's love for her adopted son. She would curse him if he abandoned his charge and the once lonely, orphaned boy came to harm. Alicia would rather lose her own life than risk Gavner's.

Larten knew that he was doing the right thing. The

only thing. But he played with alternative options every night while they jogged across the countryside, and every day as he struggled to get even a couple of hours of sleep. This was the only route open to them, yet he tried to find a way around it, a loophole which he could exploit. But there wasn't one.

They sent three telegrams to Alicia, from different towns, but they didn't dare wait for a reply, so they were not sure if she had received them. Larten didn't know much about telegrams and he mistrusted the modern technology, but Gavner assured him that they were reliable. If Alicia was safe, their messages would be delivered to her.

If…

Larten worried about leading the Nazis to the woman he loved, but Randel Chayne was a more ominous, pressing threat. Once Alicia and Sylva were clear of imminent danger, they could move to another country, out of reach of the Germans. Alicia wouldn't like moving, but Larten would convince her. She knew he wouldn't ask it of her if it wasn't essential.

Gavner didn't say much while they travelled. He still thought that Larten had made the wrong call. Alicia had been a mother to him and Sylva was like a sister. He felt that the General should not have put the clan's well-being before theirs. If anything happened to them, he didn't know if he'd ever be able to forgive the orange-haired vampire.

They hit the outskirts of Paris shortly after eleven o'clock one dark, damp night. Both were dry-mouthed as they wound their way through the streets, drawing closer to the small house where Alicia and Sylva lived. They felt as if they were walking towards an area of great disaster. There was no reason for them to feel so negatively, yet neither could shake the sense that they had arrived too late.

"We'll laugh about this afterwards," Gavner chuckled unconvincingly. "When they stare at us and ask why we look so frightened, we'll seem like fools."

"I hope so," Larten muttered.

"Even if Randel Chayne found them," Gavner went on, "he wouldn't kill them unless you were present. From what you've said, he loved to torment Tanish, to see him cringe. If he was planning to hurt them, he'd wait until you were here."

Larten considered that. "If you are right, he might be waiting for us. Perhaps he started the rumour that he was looking for me in order to draw me back to Paris."

Gavner stared at Larten. His hands were trembling, but he kept them behind his back so that Larten couldn't see. "I'm ready to fight if we have to," he said.

"I know." Larten smiled fleetingly. "But if we are attacked, and Randel is by himself, it will be best if you flee with the women, to ensure their safety. Their lives are more important than mine. Leave me to deal with the vampaneze."

Gavner nodded with relief. He wasn't relieved to be spared the dirty business of fighting — he was eager to test himself in battle. But he was glad to see that Larten loved Alicia and Sylva as much as he did, to hear him proclaim that their lives mattered more than his own. Gavner had thought that Larten was cold and unloving. Now he saw that the older vampire simply hid his feelings better than the younger vampire could.

They drew closer to the house in the suburbs. The city was asleep this far out from the centre. They passed only a handful of people on the streets, and all were hurrying home to bed. The night was young if you were a vampire, but it was late for humans.

They stopped at the front door and paused for a long, nerve-jangling second. In some ways Gavner didn't want this moment to end. If the women had been attacked, the darkest discovery of their lives lay ahead of them. Once they entered, there could be no hiding from the truth. Out here they could at least hope.

"Stay alert," Larten whispered, then fiddled with the lock. The door opened and they slid inside.

It was dark, but not to their eyes. Vampires were creatures of the night and they could see clearly in the hallway. It looked no different than it had several months earlier, that evening after their walk in the park when Gavner had twice been pushed into the pond. Larten felt his heart lift. Surely, if tragedy had befallen this house, there would be signs of struggle, grief, change.

He checked the living room where Alicia had often read to him on long, wet evenings. Rows of books lined the shelves. Larten couldn't read the titles, but he knew many of them by heart. He would give three hundred years of his life to have Alicia read to him from one of the leather-bound tomes again.

Sylva's room was next. The door was ajar. Larten hesitated before pushing it open. *She might not be here*, he thought. *If she is not in her bed, it does not mean that anything is wrong. She may have gone to stay with a friend. Be calm. Do not react hysterically. Believe.*

He pushed the door and it creaked as it swung inwards. He was so certain the bed would be empty that at first he didn't see Sylva. Then, when Gavner sighed happily, he realised she was beneath the covers, lying with her back to them. Her shoulders were rising and falling slowly, and he could hear the soft sound of her breathing.

With shaky smiles the vampires withdrew and gently closed the door.

"Did you hear her breath before we went in?" Gavner whispered.

"No," Larten answered honestly.

"Me neither. My heart was beating so hard…"

They shared a rueful chuckle then edged towards Alicia's room. Larten had already decided to let the women sleep. There was no guarantee that they were safe – Randel Chayne might be waiting on the roof or in a nearby alley – but Larten didn't think there would be an attack tonight. He and Gavner would keep watch just in case, but already his fears seemed like a foolish over-reaction. It would be bad enough telling Alicia in the morning of the way they had hurried back. She would scold them for letting their imagination run wild. But if they disturbed her sleep she would be truly furious. Alicia could cut with a wicked tongue when she was irritated.

Larten almost didn't go into her bedroom, but he wanted to see her before he withdrew for the night. He was confident that he had nothing to worry about, but he needed to be certain. He also wanted to make sure that the window was secure.

Alicia's door creaked even worse than Sylva's as Larten pushed it. He couldn't recall the doors creaking so much in the past. He would have to oil them. It wasn't good to let hinges rust. Alicia normally took care of such details. Then again, she was getting old. Maybe she'd just...

The thought died unfinished as Larten walked into the middle of a horror from his very worst nightmare.

The sheets had been torn from the bed and lay crumpled on the floor. Furniture and a large vase had been shattered and were spread in fragments around the room. There was no sign of Alicia. But above the bed, scrawled on the wall in what might have been red paint but wasn't, was a series of crooked letters.

"What does it say?" Larten croaked.

Gavner didn't answer. His eyes were bulging and his mouth was hanging open.

"What does it say!" Larten barked, shaking his assistant.

Before Gavner could respond, someone spoke softly behind them.

"This is what happens to lovers of vampires."

Gavner spun round, but Larten turned slowly. While he was turning, he struggled to get himself under control. He didn't entirely succeed, but he managed to keep the worst of his distress from his expression.

Sylva was staring at the tall vampire with the orange hair, her anguished eyes open wide in the gloom of the room. She was dressed in her day clothes, not a nightdress. Larten guessed that she had been expecting them, that she'd maybe lain in these clothes for many nights, only half-sleeping, waiting for the creak of the door to tell her they were here.

"What happened?" Gavner cried, but Sylva ignored him. She had eyes only for the man who had always refused to be a father to her.

"He came in the middle of the night," she whispered. "The darkest hour, when the world was at rest. I wasn't here. I had been seeing a young gentleman. Nothing improper, I assure you, but we liked to meet when everybody else was asleep. He's an amateur ornithologist, especially interested in nocturnal creatures." She smiled crookedly. "I used to think it would be fun to introduce him to *you*."

Gavner had started to cry. Larten couldn't. *Wouldn't*. Not until he'd heard the full story. And not until he was alone. He was determined to keep his emotions in check as long as there were witnesses.

"I was coming down the street when he burst out of the house," Sylva went on, forehead creasing as she re-lived the memories. "Patrice — my young gentleman — had left me at the end of the street. He was the perfect escort and didn't want anyone to see us together, in case they got the wrong idea. So I was alone. All by myself. Defenceless.

"The killer saw me and stopped. I think he was as shocked as I was — he can't have been expecting anyone at such an ungodly hour. He considered my fate and ran a calculating eye over me. I knew that I was dead if he chose to strike.

"But he didn't. Maybe he didn't know that I was Alicia's daughter, or maybe one of us was enough for him. Either way he spared me and fled, leaving me to enter the house alone. I could smell the blood. I knew what to expect, or thought that I did. But I hadn't imagined the variety of ways that you could rip a person apart, or the writing. I never…"

She stopped and read the words again, silently this time.

Gavner reeled aside and retched against a wall. He used a sheet to wipe his chin and cover the mess. He was sobbing uncontrollably. "What did he look like?" he groaned, but both the elder vampire and the young woman ignored the question. They knew this wasn't the work of a stranger.

"Mama told me you were a vampire when I was ten years old," Sylva said. "She thought I was old enough to deal with the truth. I was fascinated. I wanted to learn more about you and maybe join your clan. Mama pushed such ideas from my head. She told me how dangerous your world was. She loved you, but she never trusted your kind. She said that you were creatures of battle... of *blood*."

Sylva pointed to the dark red stains on the wall and said bitterly, "If only she'd known how right she was."

Sylva fell silent, waiting for Larten to speak. The vampire thought for a long time, searching for words which might ease Sylva's pain, but in the end he could only shake his head. "What do you want me to say?" he asked.

"I want you to tell me you can bring my mother back from the dead!" Sylva screamed. "I want you to say there's dark magic you can use to restore her soul. I don't care if she has to return as a monster like you. I just *want. Her. BACK!*"

Sylva shrieked the words and struck his chest with her fists — she wasn't tall enough to reach his face. Larten let her vent her fury on him. Gavner watched, stunned, still weeping.

When Sylva stopped howling and threw herself away, Larten considered going to hold her. But he didn't think she wanted to be touched, at least not by him, so he nodded harshly at Gavner. The younger vampire gulped, then crouched by Sylva's side and clutched her arms. Sylva whipped away, but when she realised it was Gavner, she smiled apologetically.

"I don't blame you for this, my dear," she sighed. "But you're one of them. A vampire like *him*." She growled at Larten as if she was a dog. "You belong to his world, not mine. You can't help me, much as I know you'd like to. I must mourn for Mama alone."

"Is she... has she been buried?" Gavner moaned through his tears.

Sylva nodded. "But don't ask me where. I'll tell you one night, when you come by yourself, but I don't want *him* to know. He doesn't deserve the chance to pay his last respects."

"I am sorry," Larten said quietly. "If I could have done anything to avoid this, I would. We came as soon as—"

"Don't!" Gavner cut him short. "You know that isn't true, so don't say it." He started to ask Sylva when Alicia had been murdered, then decided there was no point. What difference did it make?

"I will find and kill the beast who did this," Larten said, but he took no comfort from the vow and Sylva didn't either. Revenge wouldn't bring Alicia back or make either of them feel any better.

"It would be too easy to tell you that I never want to see you again," Sylva said, retreating to the window, to open it and breathe fresh air. She addressed the rest of her words to him without looking round. "If you ever loved my mother, you'll keep in touch with me. I want you to visit every so often, the way you did when Mama was alive. I want to hate you for the rest of my life and be able to direct my hatred at you in person. If you're any sort of a man, you'll grant me that opportunity."

"As you wish," Larten said stiffly, then strode to the door. He paused and spoke over his shoulder. "You should move to another house. The killer might return. Perhaps another city would be—"

"I've already thought of that," Sylva snapped. "I'm leaving with Patrice soon. We would have gone earlier, but I was sure you'd return. Send Gavner to me before you go, with instructions on how we're to keep in touch."

Larten was struck by a sense of *déjà vu* but it took him a few seconds to realise why. Then he remembered how Alicia had spoken to him the day she cast him out of her life. Sylva sounded like her mother had then, only Alicia had never despised him so violently.

"Come," Larten said to Gavner, extending a hand to help him to his feet.

"Maybe I should…" Gavner looked towards Sylva uncertainly.

"No," Larten said softly. "You can come back later. For now we must leave her to herself. It is perhaps not what she needs, but it is what she desires. We have no right to deny her the solitude she seeks."

Gavner gulped, then shot Larten a look that was almost as spiteful as Sylva's. "If you'd flitted..."

Larten had meant to hide his tears until he was alone, but he wasn't able to stop them trickling down his cheeks when Gavner cast the accusation at him. The younger vampire saw the tears and stopped, astonished and dismayed. Before he could apologise, Larten scowled and spun away.

"Hurry!" he snapped as he marched down the hallway. "We must ensure that Randel Chayne is not lying in wait. You can berate me later. For now we have Sylva to defend." He smiled bitterly. "We must not neglect our *duty*." Then he was gone, never to return to that room of blood and soul-destroying loss.

PART TWO

"So often alone"

CHAPTER EIGHT

Larten Crepsley sat by himself in the Hall of Osca Velm, staring at a long list of names on a large black stone. Although he still hadn't learnt to read, he could recognise certain words. He had seen Gavner Purl write his name many times and knew what the letters looked like. If the young vampire had made the trek to Vampire Mountain for Council, he would have been registered on this list by the guards.

Larten could have searched for Gavner mentally, which would have been quicker and easier, but he preferred this method. It gave him an excuse to be by himself for a while. He had been busier than ever since returning to the mountain some months earlier. He was tired of the endless meetings, spouting the same messages over and over, arguing and cajoling, trying to convince others to join his cause. This would be his only opportunity to relax until he staggered back to his coffin at the end of the night.

He sipped from a bowl of bat broth as he slowly studied the list of names. There was a half-drained mug of ale by the bowl, and although he'd only been here for twenty minutes, this was his third helping. Larten wasn't a natural spokesman. He found it hard to lecture for hours on end to an ever-changing array of vampires. The ale helped. It loosened his tongue and revived memories of Paris. The more he drank, the angrier he grew, and the words came readily then.

Eight years had passed since Alicia had been so cruelly taken from him. On the one hand they had been long, drawn-out years of suffering and torment, nightmares of Alicia's murder, oppressive feelings of guilt. But at the same time they'd flown by. He had never been as active as he'd been since Paris. Sometimes, when he was drunk, it seemed like he'd walked in on the horror just a few weeks ago, and every awful detail would be fresh in his mind.

Larten had been desperate to kill Nazis when he left the house. Gavner blamed him for Alicia's death, and he in turn blamed the soldiers who were pursuing them. If not for the cat-and-mouse chase, he could have flitted and Alicia would be alive. Randel Chayne was the one he hated most, but the sly vampaneze was nowhere to be found. The Nazis, however, were close. They were evil, small-minded despots, only fit for butchery.

Larten once again experienced the cold hatred which he had felt twice before, as a boy when his friend Vur Horston was killed for no good reason, and on the ship when Malora was murdered, again without just cause. In that detached, dark state he wanted only to lash out at the world and crush those who had brought pain into his life. He was older and wiser than when he'd last felt this way, but that wasn't why he was able to control his anger and spare the Nazis his wrath.

It was Gavner.

"I want to kill them."

In the Hall of Osca Velm, as Larten lowered the bowl of broth and drank from the mug of ale again, it was as if Gavner was speaking now, face illuminated by the light of the open fires.

"I want to crush those damn Nazis like ants."

Larten had turned to his assistant and squinted. They'd scouted the area around the house and found no trace of Randel Chayne. Dawn was a few hours away. There was plenty of time to find and deal with the Germans. Larten had been thinking about them since he'd turned his back on the bloodstained wall, trying to decide which methods of murder to employ. But he was surprised to hear Gavner echoing his inner thoughts.

Gavner's eyes were red and his lips were twisted as he faced Larten. "We could have saved her if we hadn't been wasting our time on the Nazis. You said we had to – it was our duty – and maybe you were right. But everything's changed. If we kill them, we can focus on Randel Chayne, hunt him down and make him pay for what he's done."

"We do not have to kill them to do that," Larten said. "We could simply out-run them."

"But they deserve to be killed," Gavner snarled, fingers knotted into fists.

Larten felt the same way, but as he studied Gavner's face, the tempest in his head died down. He saw shades of himself in his assistant. The young vampire was about to make the same mistakes that Larten had made in the past. If he did, he would have to endure the guilt and shame which had tormented Larten for so many decades.

"It will not take the pain away," Larten said softly. "Killing them will not bring Alicia back. It will only lower us to Randel Chayne's level. The Nazis are without honour, but they have not harmed us. Some have wives, children, loved ones of their own. If we slaughter them, others will feel what we are feeling now."

"Good," Gavner snapped.

Larten held his gaze. "If we kill them, women will weep. Boys and girls will ask when their father is coming home and nobody will be able to answer. Innocents will suffer. We will bring misery into the lives of people who have done nothing amiss. Is that what you truly desire?"

Gavner blinked. "Of course not, but…"

"We would be doing it for ourselves," Larten said, "not for Alicia. We would take their lives to make ourselves feel better. We would become mindless animals for a time, and in the heat of the slaughter we would not have to think about our loss or the future. It would be easy. It would be a relief. But it would also be wrong."

Gavner stared at Larten miserably, fresh tears welling in his eyes. The killer's sheen had disappeared from them and Larten was proud of the way Gavner could so swiftly turn his back on monstrous temptation. He was a better man than Larten had been at that age.

"You must leave with Sylva before daybreak," Larten said, setting his dark desires behind him, triumphing over his baser instincts for the first time in his life. "She cannot stay, even for a couple of days. If Randel Chayne or the Nazis found her, they would use her to hurt us.

89

"Go to her by yourself. She will listen to you when I am not there. Rendezvous with her young beau and travel with them. Take them far away and stay with them until they are safe. I will continue to lead the Nazis astray."

"And when Sylva's safe, I'll link up with you again and we'll go after Randel Chayne." Gavner nodded fiercely.

"No," Larten said. "I must string out the game with the Nazis for as long as I can. It will be months, maybe years before I finish with them. We have to forget about the vampaneze for now." Gavner's face darkened again, but Larten chuckled bitterly. "Do not misunderstand me. We *will* find Randel Chayne. There is nowhere he can hide from us. When time is our ally, we will track him down and kill him.

"Aye," he growled. "And we might have a little *sport* with him before we tear his head from his neck. I never had much of a taste for torture, but there is a time and a place for everything.

"But not now," he said firmly. "Our obligation to the clan comes first. We will not be reckless in this matter. We are better than Randel Chayne. We will honour those who have placed their faith in us. Then, when we have our freedom, we will find the bloodthirsty cur and extract a most terrible and fitting revenge.

"Do not return to me when you part company with Sylva," Larten said, gripping Gavner's arms. "Find another master. Learn new ways to kill. Push yourself hard. Become the finest vampire you can. When it is time, I will summon you and we will take the battle to Randel Chayne and any vampaneze who sides with him. We will kill a hundred to get to him if that is what it takes."

"You won't try to find him without me?" Gavner asked lowly.

"On Alicia's blood, I swear I will not."

And on that bleak, savage note they had parted.

Larten drained the mug of ale and called for another. He hadn't drunk so much since his nights as a Cub. Back then he had enjoyed alcohol. Now he drank solely to numb his nerves and ready himself for what was to come.

A guard added a new name to the list. Larten studied the letters, but they didn't spell *Gavner Purl*. He returned to the middle of the list – he was less than halfway through – and let his eyes scroll down again. He had gone through all of these names the night before, but he planned to re-check the whole list in case he'd missed Gavner's first time round. Of course he hadn't – Gavner would have sought him out if he'd arrived – but he played along with the game. Anything to delay the moment when he must face a wave of Generals and address them like a prophet.

As he scanned the names, his thoughts wandered once more. He hadn't seen Gavner for three years after Paris. He'd spent most of that time leading the Nazis a merry dance. Then he'd been asked to rescue a few vampires who had been caught by them. Not all of the vampires in Europe had heard or heeded Mika's warning to evacuate, and the Germans had managed to ensnare some strays.

The clashes with the Nazis might have continued if not for Vancha March. The Prince kept his nose out of the messy business for a long time. Like everybody else, he figured the likes of Mika Ver Leth and Paris Skyle were best suited to this delicate business. He thought he'd only stir things up if he got involved.

But eventually the scraggly Prince lost his temper. It was clear that the Nazis were going to carry on trapping unsuspecting vampires. They hoped to use the blood of the clan to build a regiment of super-powered soldiers. Vancha decided that the time for diplomacy had passed. Without discussing it with anyone, he took matters into his own hands.

Vancha flitted to Berlin and found the base of the Nazi leader. In the dead of night, he slipped through the arrogant Führer's defences and cornered him in his bedroom. With his nails pressed to the flesh of the trembling man's throat, Vancha told him that if even one more vampire was targeted, he would return and finish the job.

A Vampire Prince would always put the needs of the clan before his own life. If self-sacrifice was required, no Prince would hesitate to offer his life for a cause he believed in. But Vancha thought the pompous Hitler was fonder of his neck than a Prince would have been and that proved to be the case. Having been threatened, he called off his troops and no vampire had been bothered since.

Mika seethed when he heard of Vancha's heavy-handed approach. When the Prince returned to Vampire Mountain, Mika confronted him and accused him of acting without regard for the consequences of his actions. The green-haired Sire March only sniffed and said, "You can't argue with success."

Once Larten was free to focus on his own affairs, he met up with Gavner and the pair set off in pursuit of Randel Chayne. They scoured the cities of Europe, asking after him, searching for other vampaneze who might know where he was. They came across five of the purple-skinned bloodsuckers over the next few years. Each denied knowledge of Randel's whereabouts and Larten believed them — when they were blooded, every vampaneze swore an oath never to lie. They would be driven out in disgrace by their colleagues if they broke that vow, even if it was to a vampire.

He knew it was irrational, but Larten hated every vampaneze now. He blamed them for Randel's existence. If they hadn't broken away from the clan, there would never have been a Randel Chayne, or any inhuman monster like him. Alicia would be alive. Wester's family wouldn't have been killed. Tanish Eul might have never cut himself off from the clan. Larten came to believe that Wester had been right all along — the world *would* be better off without the purple scum, and Larten hoped to rid the planet of more than just a few of them.

But Randel was the one Larten hated most. If he fought with every vampaneze he met, he would be killed sooner rather than later — you couldn't cheat the odds indefinitely. Since he didn't want to die without avenging Alicia's murder, he held his tongue when in the presence of those he despised. He treated them with respect and asked politely about Randel Chayne. He said that he wished to challenge Randel because he had heard noble things about him. He gave no hint of his real reason for wanting to face the killer.

Four of the vampaneze responded with cool respect to his enquiries and let him go about his business without interfering. Only one objected and told him he had no right to answers. That vampaneze had been young and headstrong. He was eager to kill a vampire and thought Larten was the perfect place to start.

He misjudged horribly. Their duel was a one-sided contest and Larten killed the vampaneze, barely having to stretch himself. He didn't celebrate the killing, but he did sleep with a sneering smile for a few nights afterwards.

As the years turned, Larten realised he might as well be a blind man casting stones into the sea in the hope of hitting a fish. If Randel Chayne didn't want to be found, there was no way of finding him. Like those of the clan, the vampaneze could dwell in the darkest shadows of the night for centuries on end, hidden from the eyes of even the most keenly sighted.

He had hoped that other vampaneze would lead him to Randel, but the vagabonds had no spiritual homeland. They didn't gather for Council. There were no leaders keeping track of their movements. It was possible for one of them to go decades without bumping into another of his kind.

"We have to draw him out," Larten said to Gavner one dark and frosty night as they huddled over a fragile fire in a graveyard. They'd been discussing the matter in depth, both having reached the conclusion that they were on a fool's errand.

"How?" Gavner asked.

"*War*," Larten said heavily, and when their eyes met, Gavner saw that Larten hated more strongly than he ever could. In that moment he knew he didn't want to follow where Larten intended to lead. He also understood that Larten didn't want to go in that direction either. But he would. Because, unlike Gavner, he was willing to let himself become one of the truly damned if that was what it took.

Larten set off in search of Wester that night. Gavner didn't travel with him. There had been no argument. He told Larten that he'd team up with him again if either of them got a sniff of Randel Chayne, but he didn't want to be part of the General's new, tyrannical quest. Larten had accepted his assistant's decision with a curt nod. He might even have been relieved, though he gave no indication either way. With a short handshake, he turned his back on the man who had once longed to call him father and set off through the snowy recesses of the night, alone.

"So often alone," Larten muttered, staring into the dregs of his mug. He was surprised to see that he'd drained it while reminiscing.

He gazed at the remains of the ale, recalling

the many lonely years, wondering if solitude and unhappiness were always to be his lot. Then, conscious that Wester would be waiting for him, he downed the last drop, cast his eye over the most recent additions to the list to make sure Gavner's name hadn't been added, then stood and staggered from the Hall of Osca Velm, readying himself for the ignoble business of warmongering.

CHAPTER NINE

Wester had welcomed Larten into the fold without any reservations. Larten thought his old friend might try to dissuade him when he said that he wanted to help lead the clan into war, that Wester would tell him to take more time and only make a decision when his head was clear. But Wester knew what it was like to lose loved ones to the vampaneze. He didn't question Larten's reasons for joining him. Instead he simply told the General how he planned to win back supporters who had deserted them in recent years, and persuade others to unite behind them.

Larten's stock had continued to rise since they'd last spoken. Many vampires had heard about Alicia and they admired the way he'd put duty before his thirst for revenge. The pair found an attentive audience wherever they travelled. It didn't matter that Larten was a poor speaker, or that he only repeated things that Wester and others like him had been saying for decades. When Larten spoke, vampires listened, and when he asked for their support, many gave it willingly.

They'd met dozens of vampires in the course of their travels, but Council was their first chance to make a deep impression. This was when the great and the good gathered in the wintry wilds of Vampire Mountain, when they could potentially bend hundreds of Generals to their cause. Wester thought it would take thirty or forty years to win over the majority of vampires – Larten would need to become a Prince before they could push ahead with their more elaborate plans – but if they had a successful run at Council, it might be possible to do it sooner than that.

It wasn't the best time to try and promote a war. The Nazis had driven the world to global chaos. Millions of humans were locked in battle and it looked as if it would produce the highest body count ever. Many vampires thought that the Great War could not be topped, but those with first-hand knowledge of the Nazis were glumly betting on this one being even grislier.

A lot of vampires were sick of war. They'd already seen some of the casualties, towns razed to the ground, innocents rounded up and slaughtered. They wanted to retreat from battle, hole-up in Vampire Mountain for the duration of Council and pretend they lived in a civilised world.

Larten and Wester ignored all of that and worked hard to win support. They made dire predictions and grand promises, doing all in their power to convince the rest of the clan to follow them into an all-out, decisive war with the opposing creatures of the night.

They regularly focused on Mr Tiny's warning and the threat the clan faced if they did nothing. Wester even asked Larten to use the spectre of the new World War to drum up anti-vampaneze sentiments.

"If the other countries of Europe had acted earlier, the threat of the Nazis could have been nipped in the bud," Larten argued a dozen times a night. The words were Wester's (he would never have used such an expression) but he delivered them from the heart. "They have taken the world to war, but only because they were allowed to. If we do nothing, a Hitler of the vampaneze will come along and then we will face a war of *their* making. We must act now, while we have the power to control our fate. Better we start a war we can win, than find ourselves in the middle of one we are destined to lose."

Larten spoke often of his meetings with Desmond Tiny, elaborating and adding details at Wester's suggestion. He told them Mr Tiny wore a string of shrunken vampire heads around his neck. That the little meddler spoke with great fondness of the vampaneze.

That he had perched on the grave of Perta Vin-Grahl and vowed that all vampires would be buried under ice by the end of the century.

Larten didn't like lying. It went against all of his principles. And he was bad at it. But as Wester kept telling him, vampires – especially the younger members – were coming to him for horror stories. They *wanted* to hear tall tales of Mr Tiny's treachery. They *needed* to be afraid, to have a bogeyman to obsess about.

"Everything gets distorted when stories are told," Wester said. "All legends and myths are one-tenth truth, nine-tenths exaggeration. It doesn't matter if we change the facts to make more of an impact. All story-tellers have done that since the beginning of time."

Seba Nile was worried about his ex-assistants. Wester had been trying to start a war with the vampaneze for almost as long as he'd been part of the clan. Seba had never thought it would come to anything, that the guard would eventually discard his plans when he saw that most vampires were against him. But Larten had revived Wester's enthusiasm and was drawing more supporters to their dark cause with every passing night.

Seba knew that Larten sought war merely to force Randel Chayne out of hiding. He was sure Larten would regret his course in the future if he succeeded in driving the clans into battle. He wanted to sit down with the younger vampire and discuss the matter sensibly, reason with him, talk him out of his self-destructive mission.

But Larten had avoided Seba since returning. The quartermaster thought Larten knew of his ex-master's feelings and was too ashamed to talk with him one-to-one. It upset Seba that Larten should think that way, but the General was his own man and had been for a long time. It was no longer Seba's place to lecture him. He had come to believe, over the course of his many centuries, that you had to give the young the freedom to make their own mistakes.

Vancha March, on the other hand, held no such belief. He'd been abroad for the last few years, ensuring no vampires got mixed up with the Nazis. He hadn't heard about Larten's involvement with Wester, or the way they were trying to manipulate the clan.

Vancha was in high spirits when he sighted the snow-capped Mountain after a long, hard trek. Arrow was to be initiated at Council and Vancha looked forward to welcoming a new Prince into the ranks, especially one who had fallen into a pit of despair and come so close to losing everything. He might even break his own strict rules and drink a mug of ale in Arrow's honour when he was presented as a Prince to the Stone of Blood.

His excitement was quashed before he reached the network of tunnels and Halls. As he was scaling his last stretch of mountain he ran into Kurda Smahlt, a young General who had established his reputation as a thinking man's vampire. Kurda was keen to re-establish contact with the vampaneze and debate their differences. Many vampires distrusted the slim, fair-haired pacifist. Some felt he would have been better off becoming a vampaneze if he liked them so much. But Vancha had met Kurda a few times and been impressed. He didn't see eye to eye with Kurda on everything, but he thought the General was honest and intelligent, a credit to the clan.

Kurda had checked in with the guards of Vampire Mountain a few weeks before and had only ducked outside now to draw fresh air. He was in a gloomy mood when Vancha found him and the Prince soon learnt why. He was surprised to hear that Larten had sided with Wester, then angered when Kurda explained about Randel Chayne and told him some of the wilder claims which Larten had been making about Desmond Tiny.

"I don't mind a serious discussion," Kurda sighed, "but they're using lurid scare tactics to stir things up."

Vancha was supposed to announce himself to his fellow Princes as soon as he arrived, but he was so agitated by what he'd heard that he tracked down Larten and Wester first, trailed by a fascinated but nervous Kurda Smahlt. The General had never seen Vancha this worked up and wasn't sure what the Prince planned to do when he found the pair of conspirators.

Vancha located them in the Hall of Sport dedicated to Oceen Pird. Larten had been sparring. He always drew a crowd when he sparred — everyone had heard the rumours that he was edging ever nearer to becoming a Prince, so they wanted to catch him in action. Wester had been using that interest in Larten to promote their cause. Once Larten's bouts came to a conclusion, the orange-haired General would move among the excited crowd, share a barrel of ale with them and repeat his anti-vampaneze messages in an attempt to win them over.

Vancha kept to the rear for a time, listening to Larten speak of Mr Tiny, the threat of the vampaneze, the need to organise against them. The Prince's ears reddened as he listened. When he'd heard enough, he thrust through the vampires clustered around Larten and Wester.

"Crepsley!" he shouted.

"Sire March," Larten beamed, delighted to see his old friend again. He hadn't noted Vancha's angry expression, so he bowed low with a welcoming smile.

"I was not sure which of the Princes was going to be absent from this Council. I am glad it is not you. We have much—"

"What's this rubbish about going to war with the vampaneze?" Vancha snorted and Larten's smile disappeared.

"Sire?" Larten muttered. The other vampires sensed trouble and drew back. Only Wester stayed close to Larten, ready to defend him if required.

"Kurda told me you were one of Wester's puppets, but I had to see it for myself to believe it," Vancha jeered.

Larten stiffened. "I am no one's *puppet*," he growled.

"You must be," Vancha insisted. "I've known you for a long time and I've never heard you criticise the vampaneze before. Everything you're saying has come straight from the lips of Wester Flack."

"It doesn't matter where the truth originates," Wester said heatedly. "I help Larten with his speeches, but so what? Many a Prince has relied on help from his advisors. Most of our leaders aren't natural orators. Sometimes they need guidance when it comes to wording what they feel in their heart."

"No," Vancha said. "We need help wording laws and decrees, but no vampire of good standing ever needed another to tell him what was in his heart. If Larten believed what he was saying, I'd have no quarrel with him. You have your view of the world, Wester, and you're entitled to it, as every vampire is. But Larten's passing off your opinions as his own and that stinks. I won't stand for it, even if these idiots will."

He spun and glared at the vampires around them. Most dropped their gaze and coughed with embarrassment.

"You do not know what I feel or why I say these things," Larten snarled.

"Of course I do," Vancha retorted. "Your mistress was killed by a vampaneze."

"She was not my *mistress*," Larten thundered, squaring up to the Prince. "She was a gentle, loving woman, deserving of respect. I will not have you say anything derogatory about her."

"I'm not sure what that word means, but I can guess," Vancha sniffed. "I meant no offence. I'm sure she was a fine person. But no individual is worth going to war over. Find the cur who killed her and tear him apart, but don't pledge yourself to a cause you don't believe in. Don't let Wester use you as his mouthpiece. You're better than that."

"I speak the truth as I see it," Larten hissed. "The vampaneze are scum and it is time we dealt with them. If you believe otherwise, so be it. But do not try to stop me speaking my mind or treat me like a fool."

"But you *are* a fool," Vancha said and many of the vampires around them gasped.

Larten's face paled. "Take that back," he whispered.

"I won't," Vancha huffed. "You want to guide the clan to disaster because of a private feud. You seek to stir up war with the vampaneze simply because you haven't been able to find the one who hurt you — kill them all to destroy just one. Only a fool seeks war over a petty, personal cause, and I've no time for fools."

Larten was quivering with rage. "If you were not a Prince…"

"Don't let that stop you," Vancha said with a vicious grin.

For a moment Larten held back. Then, with a roar which had been building inside him since Alicia was killed, he threw himself at Vancha and lashed out.

Larten's fist connected with Vancha's chin and the Prince went sprawling. He crashed through a group of vampires and they tumbled around him like skittles, yelping with surprise.

Larten was on Vancha before the Prince could rise, punching, kicking, keen to cause maximum damage. He was normally a refined fighter and would never strike an opponent who had been knocked down. But he had lost all self-control. It wasn't the same as when he'd killed the foreman, Traz, or the people on the ship. On those occasions he had become an ice-cold killing machine. This time he simply exploded and lashed out like a child throwing a fit.

Vancha protected his face from the worst of Larten's blows while his head was spinning. The damage to his stomach and chest didn't bother him, but he couldn't let Larten strike his chin cleanly again, as another direct shot might put him out of action. He could have crawled away, but retreat wasn't in his nature. So he lay still, let Larten tear into him, and waited for his ears to stop ringing and his vision to clear.

As Larten threw one wild punch after another, Vancha's senses returned. He shook his head to steady himself, then lashed out at Larten's stomach with one of his filthy bare feet. He connected and drove the General back several steps.

Vancha was up in an instant. He spat blood, wiped the back of a hand across his lips and smiled. He made a *Come on!* gesture with his bloodied fingers and Larten swallowed the bait. Bellowing angrily, he ducked his head and charged, forgetting his decades of training.

Vancha let Larten tackle him, but before the General could wrestle the Prince to the floor, he drove a knee up into Larten's stomach. As Larten spasmed, Vancha crashed an elbow down over the back of his head. Larten slumped and rolled away, groaning.

The vampires around them cheered, even Kurda, who normally frowned upon savage battles like this. Only Wester darted towards Larten, concerned for his friend. Before he got near, someone caught his arm and dragged him back. Wester turned on his assailant furiously, only to find Seba Nile staring at him calmly.

"I came as soon as I heard," Seba said. "I would not have missed a fight between these two even if I had been on my deathbed."

"We have to help him," Wester gasped. "Vancha's mad. If we let this go on, he might—"

"If you interfere, Larten will hold it against you forever," Seba interrupted. "I almost wish I could let you make such a mistake, to drive him out from under your influence. But I know how much you care for one another and I could not bear to see your friendship end in such an ugly fashion. Leave him be, Wester. He chose this fight and he must bear the punishment if he loses."

Wester groaned with frustration, but his old master was right. For a moment he'd thought as a human, not a vampire. He felt responsible for placing Larten in this position, but ultimately it was Larten's choice to fight. He wouldn't thank Wester for trying to protect him from himself.

Vancha waited patiently as Larten staggered to his feet. The Prince could have finished off his opponent while he was vulnerable, but that wasn't his style. When the scarred General finally looked up and focused — albeit with a pair of blurry eyes — Vancha again made the *Come on!* gesture.

Larten didn't rush this time. The blow to his head had knocked some sense back into him. Taking deep breaths, he circled closer cautiously. When he came within range, Vancha struck at Larten with his right foot, testing the dazed General's reflexes.

Larten slapped the foot away and responded with a kick of his own. He hit the side of Vancha's head, but it was only a grazing blow. While Larten's leg was in the air, Vancha slipped in close and threw short, snappy punches at Larten's chest. He struck seven or eight times. Both vampires heard bones snap, but neither knew how serious the damage might be. Neither cared. Each would go on until he could fight no longer, regardless of his injuries.

Not worrying about the possibility that a shattered bone might pierce his heart or lungs, Larten kicked at Vancha again. It was similar to his last attack, and once again Vancha darted in to pound the General's chest.

But Larten had tricked the Prince this time. As his opponent came forward, Larten's other leg swung up from the floor and smashed into Vancha's side.

The Prince felt his left arm break, along with one or two of his ribs. With a cry of pain he tumbled aside. As he rose, Larten smirked and made a cynical *Come on!* gesture of his own.

Vancha grimaced, then laughed — he'd deserved that rebuke. He ignored the pain and hurled himself at Larten, throwing a series of punches and chops, a deadly force even one-handed. Larten met the Prince's assault head-on, blocking as many of the blows as he could, countering with some of his own. Both vampires stood toe-to-toe, punching, chopping, kicking, their hands and feet a blur, too fast for most of the cheering crowd to follow. Even by the standards of the clan, this was a fierce and furious fight.

Larten's face was ripped open in a number of places and he felt bones snap in his hands and feet. He was inflicting similar damage on Vancha, but the Prince had the advantage, even without the use of his left arm. As quick as Larten was, Vancha had always fought without a weapon. He'd never resorted to a knife or sword, so he knew more hand-to-hand tricks than the General. He wasn't faster or stronger, but smarter and more experienced, and that soon began to tell.

One of Larten's eyes swelled shut. A couple of his teeth tore loose and stuck in the back of his throat. It was almost impossible to breathe and he could feel his right leg about to give beneath him. Another few blows and he would be done for.

In desperation, Larten threw everything into one last kick. Creating a sliver of space for himself, he sprung into the air and launched his left foot at Vancha's head. Vancha almost didn't spot the incoming leg in time. But even a fraction of a second was enough for a vampire of his calibre to react, and he managed to drive an elbow into the leg and misdirect it. A bone snapped loudly and Larten fell to the floor in agony.

Vancha started after his opponent, then realised Larten was finished. He paused to blow blood from his nose and press his left ear back into place — Larten had almost ripped it loose. It had been a long time since the Prince had suffered such a beating, but he relished the pain. It made him feel alive.

"Had enough?" he gasped, standing over Larten, wary in case the battered General was faking.

"I... can't... go... on," Larten wheezed, only barely able to make out the shape of the burly Prince.

"Are you a fool?" Vancha asked.

Larten sneered through his pain. "*No.*"

Vancha smiled. "Then I apologise for calling you

one." He sighed and held his sides as his smile faded. "I think it's best you stay out of my way for a while. And don't let me hear you talking up war with the vampaneze again, at least not during Council. You can say what you like when I'm not around, but while I'm here, I expect silence from you on this matter."

"I will... always... obey... the wishes... of a... Prince," Larten groaned.

Vancha nodded, then hobbled out of the Hall. Vampires crowded around him to offer their congratulations, but he waved them away with a snap of his hand. He wasn't proud of himself. He should have handled this discreetly. He had lost his temper and forced a duel, where a carefully phrased warning might have sufficed. Paris would give him a stern dressing-down for this, and the ancient Prince would be right to chastise him.

In the Hall of Oceen Pird, Wester hurried to his wounded friend and asked if he needed help. Larten shook his head. He just wanted to lie there and mull over Vancha's aggressive motives. He didn't feel any shame in losing to a vampire like Vancha March. But as he lay on the floor, breathing shallowly, a mess of broken bones, cuts and bruises, he was troubled that Vancha had felt the need to pick a fight with him in the first place. He must have done something truly unpardonable to enrage the Prince, whom he had always counted as one of his closest friends.

As Larten's blood seeped into the cracks between the stones, and as pain drove him to the point of unconsciousness, he forced himself to stay awake and strained to judge his actions over the past few years, in an effort to understand what he'd done that could be considered so terribly wrong.

CHAPTER TEN

Larten recovered slowly, nursed by Wester and Seba. The old quartermaster insisted Larten be brought to his quarters, where he could keep an eye on him. Seba laid Larten in an oversized coffin and stood watch over him for the next forty-eight hours. He knew from experience that this was the most dangerous period. If any of Larten's internal organs had been seriously damaged, it should show within the first couple of nights.

Larten was unconscious for most of that time. He didn't fight sleep when it tried to claim him. He was in agony every moment that he was awake. His only comfort came when he drifted off into the land of dreams.

The vampires who had seen the fight were still talking about it. Though there would be many duels to look forward to during Council, none would be fought as passionately as this one. Those who hadn't been present were jealous and eagerly pried more details from the lucky few who'd borne witness.

Larten's defeat hadn't shamed him in any way. It was widely acknowledged that Vancha was probably the most accomplished fighter in the clan. The Generals who had seen them duel were impressed by how close Larten had come to victory, how he'd absorbed so many blows without flinching, how he'd almost been able to match the Prince. His star continued to rise even in defeat, and for that Wester was grateful.

As the nights passed, Larten improved and Seba and Wester left him to his own devices — both were manically busy in the run-up to the Festival of the Undead. Larten spent his solitary time thinking about Vancha's reasons for challenging him and how he should respond. He had rarely devoted much time to considering the future. He usually just reacted to whatever destiny placed in his path.

Now that he was incapacitated, he analysed his recent behaviour, trying to see himself as Vancha had seen him. He began to understand what he should do, the cause to which he needed to dedicate himself. He didn't discuss the issue with Seba or Wester. He wasn't sure either would agree with his assessment or approve of his plans, and he didn't wish to engage in a heated debate with them. But he needed to discuss it with

someone. Gavner Purl would have been his first choice,
but the young vampire still hadn't shown for Council
and Larten now doubted that his assistant would come
— he had the feeling that Gavner was avoiding him.
But finally a visitor arrived who was just as good a
sounding board as Gavner, and in certain ways even
better.

"I wish I'd been there to see you get pulped." Arra Sails
chuckled harshly.

Larten propped himself on an elbow and smiled
at the dark-haired vampiress. She was leaning against
the wall inside the entrance to Seba's cave, dressed
in the white shirt and beige trousers which she had
favoured for as long as he'd known her. She looked
even tougher than when he'd last seen her. Arra had
built a proud name for herself. It was doubtful that
she would ever be nominated for the highest position
— there had never been a Vampire Princess, and
though many accepted that a woman would probably
lead the clan one night, it was not yet time for such
an upheaval. But Arra was well on her way to
becoming a General of high standing, one who would
be listened to carefully by the Princes.

"I did not know you were so eager to see me fail,"
Larten said.

"After you scorned me in Germany?" she pouted. "I only wish Vancha had broken that damn neck of yours, so I could use your head as a punching bag."

It took Larten a few seconds to realise she was joking. As he smiled, she came forward and asked how he was feeling.

"Better," he said. "I have made a solid recovery. My bones are mending cleanly and I should be on my feet in time for the Festival of the Undead."

"I thought you might have planned to sit it out," Arra remarked.

"Never," Larten said. "If Vancha had broken both my legs, I would have crawled. If he had snapped my fingers, I would have used my teeth to drag myself along. I will be there and I will face anyone who wishes to challenge me."

"There will be a long line," Arra warned him. "Everyone wants a piece of the General who almost beat Vancha March."

"It was not that close a contest," Larten said. "I gave a good account of myself, but he took control early in the bout and was never in real danger of losing."

"That's not how the spectators tell it. According to them, you only lost by a whisker."

"Then they are fools," Larten grunted.

"That's what I told them." Arra perched on the edge

of his coffin and studied his bruises, still purple and tender. "Can you tell me what it was about? There are all sorts of rumours. Some claim that the pair of you were fighting over *me*."

Larten frowned. "Why should we be fighting over you?"

Arra punched his arm and he yelped. "I'm not *that* unattractive," Arra growled.

"I never meant to give the impression that you were," Larten said swiftly, turning on his old Quicksilver charm. "I was smitten from the first time I saw you. Dreaming of your beauty brings joy and warmth to my long, dark nights."

"Stop before I get sick," Arra jeered.

Larten stroked Arra's cheek and smiled fondly. Then he sighed and told her why Vancha had goaded him into battle. He was open with her and explained how he had been trying to provoke vampires, talking up war with the vampaneze, lying at Wester's prompting.

"Vancha will tolerate many indiscretions, but never a lie," Larten said soberly. "And he is right not to. It is the lowest of crimes. Anyone can make a mistake and act vilely in the heat of the moment. For that reason a crime of passion can often be forgiven. But only a person of truly low character knowingly twists the truth. Such a person can carry on in that manner for years, even decades, and bring great discredit to the clan. Vancha had every right to be angry. I am only surprised that no one reacted before him."

"They admire you too much," Arra said. "Sometimes, when you love or respect someone, you mistake their lies for truth. Most vampires don't question their leaders. If Vancha or Paris Skyle said that the sun was no longer harmful, many Generals would walk by daylight to their death, simply because they accept anything that a Prince says.

"So," she added, "does this mean you're putting thoughts of war behind you?"

Larten shook his head. "I still despise the vampaneze and believe that war is necessary if we are to safeguard our future. But I realise now that I am not a politician. I always knew that, but I let Wester convince me otherwise. Vancha did not attack me because of my beliefs, but because I was not being true to myself.

"I will do no more campaigning," Larten said. "I will make it clear that I still approve of Wester, and if anyone asks, I will tell them he has my full support. But I will not try to convince others to rally to his cause. I am not meant for such a role. Wester will not like that, but it is time I followed a path of my own choosing. I will let him use my name if he thinks there is profit in it, but I will no longer push directly for war by his side."

"What do you plan to do instead?" Arra asked.

"Hunt and fight," Larten said grimly. "It is what I should have done all along. Randel Chayne killed Alicia and he is the one I must focus on. I will scour the world for him, track down every vampaneze I can find, ask after him and challenge each to a duel."

Arra frowned. "Why the challenge?"

"To be truthful. No vampaneze would tell me about Randel if they knew that I had hidden motives for seeking him. I lied to those I spoke with before, and pretended I simply wanted to duel with Randel. I will not lie again. By being open, I hope they in turn will be open with me. By giving them the opportunity to kill me in a fair fight, I will be giving them the chance to protect Randel Chayne. I think they will respect my honesty, and if anyone knows where he is, I hope that they will tell me, seeing that I am a man of honour."

"It could be a long quest," Arra noted. "If he doesn't wish to be found, it will be hard to unearth him. You might have to fight a string of vampaneze."

"Aye," Larten sighed. "But it is the right thing to do. A vampire should never turn his back on a path simply because it is difficult. A General of good standing does not look for shortcuts."

"What if you die in one of your challenges?" Arra asked.

"Then that will have been my destiny."

Arra stroked Larten's cheek as he had stroked hers. "You speak like a Prince."

He shook his head. "I do not think I am cut from such noble cloth. I am just a man who has made many mistakes and is doing his best to make no more."

Arra sighed. "I might be about to make a mistake of my own, but if so, so be it." She trained her gaze on Larten and said, "It is time for us to mate."

Larten grinned — he thought that she was joking. But when her gaze didn't waver, his grin crumbled. "You cannot be serious."

"I said that I would take you for a mate one night," she reminded him.

"But why now?" he spluttered.

"There might not be a chance later. If Randel Chayne continues to evade detection and you fight as you mean to, one vampaneze after another, you will be defeated within a matter of years. Even the greatest warrior will fall if he engages in an endless series of battles. If we do not mate now, we might never have the opportunity."

"It is too soon," Larten said. "I think about Alicia all of the time."

"I'm not asking you to forget her," Arra snapped. "And I don't care if you don't love me. Most vampires don't love in the way that humans do — we live too long for such follies of the heart. All I'm asking for is a seven-year contract. Be my partner. Let me hunt and fight with you and be your second in duels. Let me cleanse your wounds when you are injured and dispose of your remains in a fitting manner if you are killed.

"We complement each other," she continued. "We see the world in a similar way. I can learn from you and you can draw comfort and support from me. In seven years, if we're both alive and have had enough of one another, we can go our separate ways. Better that than we never mate and wonder for the rest of our lives what it might have been like if we'd tried."

Larten blinked. "You would never make a great romantic," he noted wryly.

"I don't want to be," Arra said. "I'm a vampire, a warrior, a creature of the night. And, if you think highly of me, I will be your mate."

"I *do* think highly of you," Larten said softly. "And I would be proud to pledge myself to you. So if you are certain that Mika will not object…"

"I wouldn't care if he did," Arra smirked. And then, leaning into the coffin, she wrapped her arms around Larten and kissed him, locking her lips on his, pledging herself to him with all of her spirit. Some of his wounds reopened as she hugged him and he tasted blood in his mouth, but he didn't care. The pain of love was no real pain at all.

Later that night, in the presence of Seba, Wester and Mika Ver Leth, Larten faced Arra over his coffin and spoke softly but firmly. "I ask that you be my mate for the next seven years. I vow to be faithful during that time. I will fight in your name, do all that I can to honour you, and die for you if required. I will claim no hold over you once the contract has elapsed. Do you accept my terms?"

"I do," Arra said simply.

To a chorus of cheers they kissed again, and in that moment the mating ritual was concluded. It might not have been the most romantic night of Larten's life, but it was without doubt one of the happiest.

PART THREE

"Randel Chayne can damn well wait"

CHAPTER ELEVEN

When Larten left Vampire Mountain shortly after the end of Council, he knew he wouldn't return in the near future, as he didn't want to get mixed up in Wester's political games. But he had no idea that it would be almost half a century before he'd gaze upon the peak of the great mountain again. If he had known, he might have paused to glance back and savour the sight. But probably not. He was a vampire, and the children of the night had little patience for sentimental nonsense.

The next few years were a bloody time, both for Larten and the world. He and Arra crossed an endless array of grisly battlefields which had scarred the soil of so many countries. Even the war-weary Larten had never seen such mounds of corpses before, or watched humans fight so savagely, destructively, inhumanly.

They encountered almost no vampires in their travels. The members of the clan wanted nothing to do with the atrocities. This was not war as they knew it — it was plain, bloody butchery.

Larten sometimes wished that Vancha hadn't just threatened the Nazi leader, but killed him when he had the chance. Maybe this could have been avoided if the vampires had been harsher. Nobody had predicted a war on such a scale, but they'd guessed that the Germans would drag the world into battle. Perhaps they should have done more to prevent this from coming to pass.

Arra argued against that when he told her of his thoughts. "We can't intervene in the affairs of humans," she said. "We put their ways behind us when we were blooded. Humans and vampires were not meant to mix. If we involved ourselves in their problems, more would learn of our existence and that would lead to trouble. Millions would want to be blooded, to enjoy long lives and extra strength. But they wouldn't care about honour or our laws. They'd only want power. If we refused their advances, they'd seek to destroy us, so that we couldn't enjoy what had been denied to them."

It was the old argument for why vampires didn't meddle and it was as valid now as it had always been. But Larten still sometimes studied the ruined landscape and wasted lives, and wondered.

One thing he never wondered about was his quest. Randel Chayne had crossed all lines of decency and deserved to be punished. It didn't matter to Larten that so many others were committing even worse crimes than Randel's. He couldn't solve all of the problems of the world and he wasn't fool enough to try. But he *could* do all in his power to make sure that the rogue vampaneze paid for what he had done.

Larten made no headway for a long time. The vampaneze, like the vampires, were keeping their heads down during the calamitous war, harder to locate than ever. Larten only found two in the first couple of years. Both accepted his challenge and died at his hand, but neither knew anything of Randel Chayne.

With the third he got his first sniff of a break, though in many ways he wished that he had never met this particular vampaneze at all.

Her name was Holly-Jane Galinec and she was a few decades older than Larten. She was the only female of her breed that he had ever encountered. The vampaneze were even stricter with new recruits than vampires were and almost never admitted a woman into their ranks. Holly-Jane must have been a warrior of high standing for them to have accepted her as an equal.

But Holly-Jane's nights as a warrior were behind

her. She was holed-up in an under-fire city when Larten tracked her down and her left leg had been blown off at the knee. She was waiting for the battle to end, planning to drag herself out of the rubble to seek an honourable death. She was delighted when Larten confronted her. She had assumed that she would have to perish in a fight with a pack of vile Nazis. The chance to die at the hands of a vampire filled her with glee.

"It must be fate!" Holly-Jane kept whooping as they drank from a bottle of wine which she had been holding back for a special occasion. She was living beneath the streets, where bombs couldn't strike, and had only left her den in recent months to feed.

"I drank from the dead," she explained. "It would have been wrong to kill one of the living when there are so many corpses lying around. It's not our way to feed without killing, but in this crazy time I felt it would be unjust to add to the woes of these poor people."

Larten could see that Holly-Jane must have been a good-looking woman once, pretty in a tough way, like Arra, but now she was filthy and wild-eyed. Disease had eaten into the stump of her leg and she'd had to cut it shorter on four different occasions. "Or was it five?" she mused aloud, studying what was left of her thigh. "I had to get drunk – the pain would have been too much to bear otherwise – and I think I may have operated twice one time. I get carried away when I'm excited."

Although they were not overly sympathetic by nature, Larten and Arra felt sorry for the fallen vampaneze. She had a cheerful manner, which was uncommon for one of her kind. They didn't want to like the one-legged wreck, but instinctively found themselves warming to her.

It took Larten a few hours to tell Holly-Jane of his mission. When they first discovered her in her putrid hole beneath the earth, Holly-Jane wept with joy and insisted they dine with her and share her wine. Larten tried to explain about his quest, but Holly-Jane waved his explanation away and said it could wait. "It's not like I'm going anywhere soon," she quipped. Not wanting to refuse her hospitality, they chewed on the stale bread and scraps of rancid meat that she had saved up, and pretended to savour the disgusting wine.

When Larten finally broached the subject of Randel Chayne, Holly-Jane stunned him by saying, "Randel? Of course I know him. He's one of my best friends. Why are you interested in that old bear?"

For a long moment Larten couldn't respond. He and

Arra shared an astonished, sceptical look. Holly-Jane saw that they didn't believe her. She laughed and described Randel Chayne in detail. By the time she'd finished, Larten doubted no longer.

"I wish to challenge him," Larten said. "He killed someone close to me and I seek revenge. I will face him cleanly, openly. It will be a fair fight. If you wish to protect him from me, I understand, and I will not press you for—"

"No, no," Holly-Jane said quickly. "Randel loves a good fight. I'm sure he'd want me to tell you all that I know. But I fear you're too late. I was due to meet with him several years ago in Venice. Have you been there? It's my favourite city. If only I could have been trapped there instead of this cesspit!

"Anyway, Randel set a date and place. I got there early — he was always punctual and I didn't want to annoy him by arriving late. But although I waited for a month, there was no sign of him, and nobody's seen him since. I hate to admit it, but I think Randel might be beyond your reach."

Larten gawped at the invalid. He had imagined many scenarios over the years since Alicia had been taken from him, but never this. He should have considered it — the vampaneze led harsh, testing lives, and many were cut down in their prime. But he'd never stopped to think that Randel Chayne might already be dead, that destiny may have conspired to rob him of his revenge.

"Are you sure that he is dead?" Larten wheezed.

"No," Holly-Jane said. "But before my accident I met a few others who knew him. They all mentioned the fact that they hadn't seen Randel lately. I'd be very surprised if he turned up alive."

Larten began to tremble. Arra tried to think of something to say but couldn't find words that might offer any comfort. In the end Larten cleared his throat and asked Holly-Jane where Randel might have gone if he was alive, perhaps wounded like the female vampaneze.

Holly-Jane listed a number of places which Randel had frequented – Paris was one of them – then beamed. "So, are you ready for the grand finale? I'd rather fight on the surface, beneath the light of the moon, but the crawl would exhaust me and I think we should act as if I have a glimmer of a chance."

Larten didn't want to fight the one-legged vampaneze, but if he refused to duel, Holly-Jane would be disgraced. So he fought brutally and without mercy, treating the wounded warrior the same as any other opponent. Holly-Jane died with a smile on her lips and Larten truly meant it when he made the death's touch sign over her corpse and said, "You were a credit to your clan."

After they'd buried Holly-Jane, Arra glanced at the subdued Larten and said, "What now?"

Larten thought for a long time before answering. "We carry on as before. Randel might be alive. Until we have proof that he is dead, we continue."

"And if we never find proof?" Arra pressed.

Larten shrugged. "I will continue searching for Randel Chayne until I find him or until I die."

"That sounds like a waste of time to me," Arra sniffed.

Larten smiled tightly. "Many would have said that Holly-Jane was wasting her time by clinging on to life down here and suffering such indignities. But she died nobly in the end. Even if she had not, she would have been correct to stay true to her course, as I shall stay true to mine."

With that, he led Arra out of the cramped tomb and climbed back to the world of man and war, to pursue the trail of what he now feared was only the ghost of Randel Chayne.

CHAPTER TWELVE

Larten searched doggedly for the next couple of years. He tried to act as if nothing had changed, but Arra knew that he was troubled. She hadn't managed to get as close to him in their time together as she'd wished, and was sure they would part at the end of their term as mates. But she had come to understand him and could see that he was torn. He'd sworn himself to this path and was determined to see it through to the end. But at the same time he had the feeling that it was pointless. Nobody could be truly comfortable if they had to live with the possibility that they might be forced to chase shadows for hundreds of years.

Arra tried on many occasions to reason with Larten, to convince him to abandon his mission. "You don't have to give up entirely," she argued. "You can still keep an ear and eye open. If he resurfaces, head after him again. It's unlikely that he'd kill Alicia to hurt you, then disappear from your life forever. If he's alive, he'll come back to take another stab at you, like he did with Tanish Eul. That's when you should hunt for him, not now."

Larten knew that Arra was right, but he found it difficult to abandon his quest. He feared what Randel Chayne might do if he returned and struck when Larten was unprepared — he might target Arra, Wester, Gavner or Seba. The General didn't want to lose another loved one to the murderous vampaneze.

But he also wanted to carry on because he wasn't sure what he would do if he stopped. Larten had found meaning in the search. He had never felt as focused as he did now. He had come to a simple, defining point of his life — he existed to find and kill Randel Chayne. He liked having no grey areas to worry about. If he gave up, he feared a return to the times when he'd thought that his life lacked direction.

Larten fought another two vampaneze, one of whom knew Randel Chayne but hadn't seen him in over a dozen years. The one who had known Randel was a hard, experienced warrior and treated Larten to his toughest test so far. He wounded the vampire seriously and almost opened Larten's stomach with a swipe of his nails. Larten triumphed, but only barely, and Arra needed to stitch him together afterwards — their spit wasn't strong enough to close all of his wounds.

Larten spent more than a month recovering before he took to the road again. When he did, he headed for Berlin. According to Holly-Jane Galinec, that had been one of Randel's favourite cities. Larten hadn't wished to travel there while the Nazis were in control, as he didn't want to fall into their hands. But the tide of the war had turned. It was nearing its end and the Germans had been pressed back. They were only weeks away from ultimate defeat, maybe less, and Larten felt that now was as good a time as any to zone in on Berlin.

He wouldn't admit it, even to himself, but part of his reason for going there now – as opposed to waiting a few months until it was completely safe – was that he wanted to be present when the Nazis fell. He had no plans to gloat, but he would be grimly satisfied when he saw them surrender. They had put this world through hell and he was delighted that they'd failed.

The vampires made good time, skirting the areas where fighting still raged, and arrived in Berlin on a dark, cloudy night. The city had changed drastically since Larten had last visited. It was a pale ghost of its former self, shredded by bombs and bullets. Wandering the pockmarked, dusty, bloodstained streets, Larten found it hard to believe that the city could ever recover from a levelling this severe. But he knew how resourceful humans were, how swiftly they bounced back from disaster and tragedy. He was sure this would be a thriving metropolis again within ten or twenty years.

In 1945 Berlin was a city of vicious dangers, but Larten and Arra walked the streets without fear, at home among the shadows, silent as they listened to the cries, screams and gunfire which saturated the night. It was as if the great old city was dying, leaking corpses and rubble instead of blood.

Larten expected to see Desmond Tiny. He had been sighted a few times during the war, always where the fighting was thickest, cheerfully plodding through fields of blood and guts. But if he was present now, Larten saw no sign of the eternal meddler.

The General had decided to seek shelter – day was coming – when Arra touched his arm. "Look," she said, pointing at a group of people crossing a mound of bricks and timber in the distance.

Larten studied the people, but couldn't see how they were different to the many other refugees he had spotted over the course of the night.

"The one carrying the woman and child," Arra prodded him.

Larten squinted, but couldn't get a fix on their faces. "My eyes are not as good as yours," he said. "Who is it?"

"You'll find out soon," Arra smirked and smugly set off ahead of him. She was always pleased when she scored points over a man, even if he was her mate.

They trailed the group across the rubble and closed in on them. Larten was able to make out their features as they drew nearer, but the man carrying the woman and child had his back turned to them. Larten guessed by the way he carried the pair so easily that he was a vampire, but he didn't know who it might be. Not Gavner – he wasn't broad – and certainly not Vancha March. He thought it might be Mika Ver Leth, but he couldn't be sure.

They caught up to the humans as they entered a ruined hospital which was still in operation, albeit only just. Canvas had been stretched across the holes in the roof and candles flickered everywhere. Larten could tell by the scents and sounds that there weren't many people inside. He paused in the doorway and glanced at Arra.

"Are you sure this is safe?" he asked.

"Absolutely." She raised an eyebrow. "Don't you recognise his scent?"

Larten sniffed the air, but it was thick with the stench of human blood. "Can you not just tell me?" he growled.

Before Arra could answer, a man said from within

the darkness, "She doesn't need to. Welcome, Larten. Greetings, Arra."

A young vampire in a muddied blue suit stepped forward. He had blond hair, a delicate face, and was of slight build.

"Kurda Smahlt?" Larten said with surprise.

Kurda smiled and bowed to the General. "The one and only. Now come on in and make yourselves at home. I'm delighted to see you both."

"Why?" Arra frowned — she had never been particularly friendly with Kurda.

"I need your spit," Kurda said, and laughed at their bemused expressions.

CHAPTER THIRTEEN

Kurda led the couple on a short tour of the makeshift hospital. There were fourteen patients, three nurses and some volunteers. Conditions were squalid, almost no medicine, hardly any bandages and few clean sheets. But every patient knew that they were fortunate. Berlin was full of the wounded and dying, people who couldn't find any form of aid, even a ward as rough as this one.

"It's chaotic at the moment," Kurda said, rubbing spit into the wound of an unconscious woman. Most of her right arm was open and festering. His spit would work only limited good on an injury this serious, but he persevered. "Everyone knows the war is lost. Surrender is the only sensible option. But the Nazis won't go easily. Thousands more will perish needlessly before the beast roars its last and is buried forever."

"How long have you been here?" Larten asked, studying the people in the beds and cots.

"A few weeks," Kurda said. "I came when I realised the end was nigh. Their leaders are wicked, warped creatures, but these are good, honest people deserving of help."

"Why do you care?" Arra frowned. "Aren't there human doctors who can look after them?"

"There will be soon," Kurda nodded. "But as I said, it's chaos now. The medics will arrive too late to save most of these patients."

"Are you from this city?" Arra asked.

"No," Kurda said.

"From Germany?"

"No."

"Then I'll ask again, why do you care?"

Kurda shrugged. "I like to help."

"I thought you'd have been too busy trying to make peace with the vampaneze to waste time on humans," Arra sniffed.

"Things have been quiet between the two clans during the war," Kurda said. "Both have withdrawn, waiting for the conflict to end, eager not to get involved. There wasn't much for me to do, so I thought I'd try to do some good here. I've been working wherever I could help. I spent a lot of time smuggling people out of Nazi-controlled territories, but in more recent times I've been focusing on casualties like these."

"Who did you smuggle?" Larten asked. "Soldiers? Politicians?"

Kurda shook his head and stopped by a bed where a man in a doctor's gown was wiping a child's fevered brow. The man was pale and unhealthy-looking, very thin, and his short hair looked as if it had been shaved to the bone in the near past. As he wiped sweat from the child's eyes, Larten noticed a tattoo on the man's arm, a series of letters and numbers.

"How is she doing, James?" Kurda whispered.

"Not good." The man glanced around. "She's fighting hard, but I think…" He sighed.

"This is James Ovo," Kurda introduced them. "He has been with me for the last couple of months. He's a good friend and a more than passable doctor."

James snorted. "I wouldn't say that."

"This is not your profession of choice?" Larten asked.

"No," James said. "I was an undertaker, like my father and grandfather. I hoped my sons would follow in our footsteps, but…" His face darkened and Kurda squeezed his shoulder.

"Have you heard of the death camps?" Kurda asked softly as they stepped away from the bed.

"Rumours," Larten nodded. "I ignored them. One hears wild tales every time there is a war."

"This time the tales are true," Kurda said. "And I

doubt if the rumours you heard came anywhere close to the truth." He started to tell them about the camps, what happened to people like James Ovo and his doomed sons. Then he stopped. This wasn't the time or place to talk of such horrors.

"Anyway," Kurda said, "I hope you'll help now that you're here. I've been doing as much as I can, but my throat feels like it's made of sandpaper. If you wouldn't mind lending a mouthful or two of spit…"

"Why should we?" Arra asked. "This isn't our war and these aren't our people. What concern are they of ours?"

Kurda grimaced, but didn't argue. Arra wasn't being insensitive. This was the way many vampires thought. They expected no help from humans in their own times of trouble and believed that humanity should therefore expect no help from the clan in theirs.

Larten, however, remembered the First World War and a night when he'd led a group of soldiers through the hell of no man's land, back to their trench. He looked back on that as the start of his recovery. After killing so many innocents on the ship en route to Greenland, he had believed for a long time that he could never make amends. He still wasn't sure that he could, but when he'd helped those soldiers, he'd felt for the first time as if there might be some small shimmer of hope for his soul. He hadn't dedicated himself to good deeds from that night on – he wasn't that sort of person – but now that an opportunity to help had presented itself, he seized it.

"Tell me what you want me to do," Larten said quietly. As Arra stared at him, he shrugged. "Friends of another vampire's are friends of mine."

Arra scowled, then sighed and worked a ball of phlegm up her throat. "Come on then, fool," she barked at Kurda. "Show us where to gob!"

They toiled until midday, sheltered from the sun inside the gloominess of the building. James Ovo and a few of the volunteers went out early in the morning and returned with another handful of injured stragglers. A couple of the patients from the night before died, while one was deemed fit enough to be dismissed.

And so the work continued.

They finally rested on rough beds in a room in the basement. Kurda apologised for not being able to provide coffins, but said he wasn't fond of them and hardly ever slept in one.

"Why doesn't that surprise me?" Arra huffed, biting into a loaf of bread which one of the volunteers had given to her. When she saw that Larten wasn't eating, she paused. "Not hungry?"

"We can thrive on blood, of which there is plenty," he said. "The humans need food to survive, and of that there is little."

Arra rolled her eyes. "I never knew you were so soft," she grumbled, but set her bread aside to be divided out among the patients.

Kurda was smiling. "It's good to see you. I thought, after Vampire Mountain, that you wouldn't want to speak with me again."

"Why?" Larten frowned.

"I told Vancha about your speeches, so I figured you might…" Kurda stopped and cleared his throat. "You knew that, right?"

"No," Larten rumbled, glaring at the vampire who'd suddenly turned a paler shade of white. But Larten couldn't maintain the pretence, and after a few seconds he laughed. "You need not worry. I deserved my thrashing. I was all the fool that Vancha said I was, and maybe more. You did me a favour by telling him, and if you had not, someone else would have."

"That's a relief," Kurda chuckled. His smile faded and he leant forward. "Does that mean you no longer support Wester Flack and his drive for war?"

Larten pursed his lips. "I think that the vampaneze are a menace and we should deal with them before they rise against us. But whipping vampires up into a fury is not for me. If war comes, I will fight gladly. If I am asked for my opinion, I will speak out in favour of Wester and those who campaign with him. But I am through with speeches. I will leave those to the professionals."

"Surely you can't crave war," Kurda groaned. "After everything you must have seen these past few years?"

"I have observed many wars over the decades," Larten replied. "Sometimes, I admit, for sport, although that was long ago when I was young and even more foolish than I am now. This war is nastier than most, but they are all brutal at the core. That is the nature of warfare."

"Yet you still believe in it?" Kurda pressed.

"It is sometimes necessary," Larten said. "It is better to defend yourself against an enemy than cave in to them. The British, French and their allies have suffered, but this was a war they had to fight."

"No," Kurda grunted. "They could have negotiated, reasoned, sought peaceful solutions to their problems."

"Reasoned with the Nazis?" Larten jeered. "You do not know these people if you think that they were ever open to *reason*."

"The Nazis didn't spring to power overnight," Kurda argued. "If the people of other countries had paid more attention and dealt with Germany's problems in the early 1920s, before the Nazis came to prominence..."

"That is easy to say now," Larten noted. "But by the time people realised that the Nazis were a threat, it was too late for diplomacy."

"I don't agree," Kurda said. "But even if that was true, it doesn't change *our* circumstances. We know that the vampaneze are a threat, but they don't currently scheme against us. We're at peace with them and we should use that lull to secure the long-term security of both clans. This is our chance to stop the threat of war at its source and ensure that we never face what these humans have had to endure."

Larten shook his head. "It sounds like a solid argument. But so does Wester's. If we go to war while the vampaneze are weak, we can slaughter them all. If, on the other hand, we allow them to flourish, they will always be a threat. There can be no real truce since we both hate what the other clan stands for."

"We can work on that," Kurda insisted. "We might find we're not so different if we sit down and talk."

"But what if we find that we are?" Larten countered. "What if those talks make us realise that there can never be a union, if your search for peace proves to be the catalyst which drives the clans to war?"

Kurda frowned. "You're a dangerous one, Crepsley. I see now why Wester tried to make you his spokesman. You have a sly tongue. I think you could convince me to change my opinions if you had long enough to work on me."

"Maybe I will," Larten smiled.

"You plan to stick around?" Kurda asked.

"No," Arra cut in, then glanced at Larten. "We're not staying, are we?"

"Actually, we are," Larten said softly. "There are people to help and a doubter to convert."

Arra blinked. "What about Randel Chayne?"

Larten considered that, then said firmly and with great satisfaction at being able to say such a thing after all these years, "Randel Chayne can damn well wait."

CHAPTER FOURTEEN

Larten and Arra stayed with Kurda for the remainder of the war in Europe, then for several months afterwards. While humans were celebrating the end of the hostilities and looking forward to a more hopeful future, the vampires were busy criss-crossing the continent, helping wherever they could. They went to places where human medics were slow to visit, areas where anarchy was rife and bullets still flew.

When they heard of the terrible bombs which had been dropped on two cities in Japan, they flitted East. There, in the ashen ruins of Hiroshima, Larten discovered a new breed of horror. His many decades had never prepared him for such total destruction. He and the others worked feverishly, as if caught in a nightmare. They couldn't do much to ease the pain of those who had been burnt and warped by the lethal bomb, but they did what little good that they could.

Larten hardly slept while in Japan. Every time he tried, his head filled with the cries of the suffering and he was unable to block out the awful things which he'd seen. Even when he closed his eyes he saw them, faces stripped of everything that made them human, charred bodies floating in the putrid water of the rivers and streams, children choking on the poisoned air.

Larten felt old and tired when they departed, as if he was a man who had lived too long. The world had changed beyond recognition and he didn't want to be part of this new, barbaric place. In his mind's eye he was still a citizen of the nineteenth century, hailing from a period when war could be noble. This was the first time he had noted a cultural chasm between the people he'd known then and those of this modern era. He now understood why older vampires like Seba and Paris Skyle tried to withdraw from the human world entirely. It wasn't just that vampires and humans were different. If you lived long enough, it began to seem as if you were part of a separate species.

Arra was eager to resume the hunt for Randel Chayne. She wanted to explore the world, hunt vampaneze, embrace the night. Though she hadn't said anything, she felt they'd been wasting their time helping humans and was keen to return to proper vampire work.

Larten's heart was no longer in his quest. He still wished to bring Alicia's killer to justice, but the thought of searching for the elusive, probably deceased vampaneze for decades to come filled him with gloom. He had enjoyed being able to make an impact while helping Kurda. Life was easy when you had direct and pressing problems to solve. Part of him was sorry that the war had ended. He missed waking with a definite agenda, never needing to look any further ahead than the next few hours.

"Where will you go?" Kurda asked as they prepared to part ways.

"Wherever the vampaneze are," Arra sniffed.

Larten said nothing and Kurda caught an uncertain look in the vampire's eyes. "You could stay with me," he offered.

"And help you make peace with our foes?" Arra laughed. "I don't think so."

"I didn't mean that," Kurda said patiently. "I received a message from Vancha. He's going to a wedding of a friend of ours. It will be a highly unusual ceremony. If you like, you can come. If nothing else, it would be a good opportunity for you to make your peace with Vancha."

Larten wasn't sure he wanted to face the Prince so soon after their fight. But it wasn't a vampire's way to run from his fears, so he nodded gruffly and said, "Very well. We will travel with you a while longer. But tell me, what is so unusual about this wedding?"

Kurda grinned. "If I told you, you wouldn't believe me!"

The wedding was scheduled to take place in a small, isolated cove. Larten, Kurda and Arra arrived a few nights before the ceremony to find Vancha March and another vampire sitting alone in the middle of a beach, eating raw crabs.

Larten recognised the other vampire even from a distance and felt a stab of pleasure shoot through him. He almost broke into a trot, but that wouldn't have been dignified, so he kept to the same deliberate pace and made sure he looked suitably serious.

Vancha heard them coming and rose to greet them. The other vampire's senses weren't as sharp and he carried on eating, poking bits of flesh out of the shells, swallowing them with evident disgust.

"I don't understand how anyone can enjoy this," the vampire grunted.

"Perhaps your senses would not be so dull if you ate more seafood," Larten said drily.

The vampire jolted with surprise, then surged to his feet. "Larten!" he cried.

"It is good to see you again, Gavner," Larten said politely, bowing to his ex-assistant.

Gavner Purl ignored the bow and hugged the orange-haired vampire. Larten looked startled. Then, with a shy smile, he patted Gavner's back.

"I've missed you," Gavner said, letting go and beaming.

"I do not know why," Larten said. "I have not missed you." But there was a twinkle to his eyes and Gavner knew that he was being teased.

Larten faced Vancha March and bowed again. "Sire," he said quietly.

"Larten," Vancha grunted, casting a critical eye over the General. "How are your ribs?"

"All healed."

"I thought you'd still be hobbling after the beating I gave you."

"I have sustained worse injuries stumbling down stairs," Larten said.

Vancha scowled. "Be careful or I'll knock you about again."

"I had been drinking when we fought," Larten said. "Sober, I do not think you would fare so well against me."

Vancha's eyes narrowed. Then he laughed and Larten chuckled too. The pair smiled at each other, their differences put behind them.

"No more nonsense about going to war with the vampaneze?" Vancha asked.

"Not for the time being," Larten replied.

"Good." Vancha bowed low to Arra. "Mistress Sails, it's a pleasure as always. You grow more radiant with every passing night."

"Save it for the fools who believe your flattery," Arra sniffed.

"She likes me really," Vancha said, nudging Gavner. "When she sees sense and abandons this orange-haired buffoon, she'll be mine."

"I'd rather mate with the frozen remains of Perta Vin-Grahl," Arra said icily.

Vancha cackled and bid Kurda welcome, then the five vampires squatted around the remains of the crabs and spent the rest of the night catching up. They slept in a cave when the sun rose. Vancha sneaked out in the middle of the day and returned with a fresh load of live crabs, which he tipped onto the sleeping Gavner. When the young vampire shot awake, yelping as the crabs pinched him, Vancha laughed until his face turned as purple as the animal skins he always wore.

"You are a cruel master," Larten tutted when the Prince had recovered.

"Gavner's no assistant of mine," Vancha responded. "We've travelled together for several months, but I've no wish to mentor any Cub right now. I keep telling him to get lost, that he's like a thorn in my side. I'm hoping he'll take the subtle hints and go his own way after the wedding."

"He is more persistent than you might imagine," Larten said.

"Maybe," Vancha said with a wicked laugh. "But I can find even bigger crabs tomorrow!"

Shortly after dusk, a man in dark brown robes made his way down to the cove and met with the vampires. His name was Laurence and he lived in a nearby monastery. He was due to wed the engaged couple and had come to check that everything was in order and ask if the guests needed anything.

"We don't have much," Laurence said, "but we keep bees and goats, so we have honey and milk. We make our own bread too, and grow a variety of herbs and vegetables. You are more than welcome to dine with us."

Not wishing to appear ungrateful, the vampires accepted Laurence's invitation and followed him to the monastery, which nestled close to the top of the cliff a bit further along the coastline. It was a small, humble building which had been battered by the elements. About thirty monks were present.

The vampires ate with the monks. It was a plain meal, but carefully prepared. Larten thought that the monks would be fascinated by their visitors — they knew that the five were vampires, and in Larten's experience, humans always wanted to learn more about the legendary creatures of the night. But the monks only made polite enquiries and didn't bother the vampires with an endless string of questions. When Larten asked Laurence about this lack of interest, he smiled.

"We don't pay much attention to the outside world," Laurence explained. "We have devoted our lives to prayer and inward reflection. To us there is little difference between your nocturnal clan and any other group."

Laurence took the vampires on a tour of the monastery after dinner and told them how the monks lived, outlining their daily routines. It was a simple but satisfying life, and Larten found himself envying them. After the horrors of the war and his brutal quest to find Randel Chayne, this seemed like an idyllic existence.

Larten noticed two men who weren't dressed in robes, scaring bats away from the fruit trees which grew in one of the monastery's plots. He asked if they were local gardeners who had been hired to help with the tasks.

"No," Laurence said. "They are part of our community, but not our order. We rarely turn anyone away. If lay people wish to come stay with us, to escape the breakneck pace of the world, find inner peace or just relax for a time, we welcome them. We ask that they work to help pay towards their upkeep, but they're not compelled to. Most only stay for a few weeks or months, but a couple have been with us for years."

"Why don't they become monks if they're here that long?" Kurda asked.

Laurence shrugged. "They enjoy our way of life, but do not necessarily share our beliefs."

"But you accept them even if their beliefs are different?" Kurda pressed.

"Of course," Laurence said. "There is room in this world for all sorts of beliefs. The most important thing is that we respect one another and create a community where all are welcome and treated equally."

"That's a nice way of looking at the world," Kurda murmured. "I wish we could all see it that way." He caught Larten's eye and raised an eyebrow.

Larten scowled, but it was an automatic response. Though he would never admit it to Kurda, he too wished the world was that way, and the more he explored the monastery, the more he yearned to leave the duties and worries of the clan behind and find the peace here which had so far eluded him for most of his life.

CHAPTER FIFTEEN

Laurence asked the vampires to stay with them the following day. Vancha didn't want to sleep in the relative opulence of the monastery, but he accepted the monk's offer so as not to offend him, then searched for the roughest, coldest floor he could find. Arra and Larten shared a room next to Kurda and Gavner on the upper floor of the building. Arra fell asleep and was soon snoring lightly. Larten dozed for a few hours, but he kept waking, thinking about the war, Randel Chayne, the monks. He had a lot on his mind and eventually he walked out onto the balcony to squint at the sea.

"Can't sleep either?" someone said from the balcony next to his. He turned to find Gavner sitting in a chair, covered by a blanket to protect him from the sun.

"I wish that I could," Larten sighed. "I have not had a good day's sleep in a *long* time."

"You didn't say much last night about what you'd seen in Japan," Gavner noted.

"It is not something I care to talk about."

"Bad?" Gavner asked softly.

"The worst." Larten scratched his scar, then massaged the back of his neck. "I sometimes think we should have stayed in Greenland and frozen. The more I see of this world, the less I find in it to admire."

"You don't mean that," Gavner said. "We had enjoyable times over the years. Paris before Tanish Eul tore us apart. When I was your assistant. Paris again when we returned, until..." He stopped.

"Randel Chayne," Larten said bitterly, then glanced at Gavner and muttered, "I think he is dead."

"Why?" Gavner asked eagerly. "What have you heard?"

Larten told the young vampire about Holly-Jane Galinec.

"I don't know," Gavner hummed. "That's hardly proof, is it?"

"No," Larten said. "And I will search until I am certain. But I sense that he is dead. I have an instinct for such things and I am rarely wrong."

"I hope he's still alive," Gavner growled. "I want to help kill him. I'll feel cheated if somebody else has beaten us to it."

Larten was surprised. "I thought you had changed your mind about that. You have avoided me in recent times. When you did not come to Council, I assumed you wished to draw a line between us."

Gavner shook his head. "I just didn't like the way you were trying to drive the clan to war. I don't hate the vampaneze – they are what they are – but I loathe Randel Chayne. If you find him, I definitely want to be there when you cut him down."

Larten was glad to see that the thirst for revenge was still strong in Gavner. But on another level he was disappointed. He had hoped that his ex-assistant would have found the capacity for forgiveness which Larten had never known.

"Have you been in touch with Sylva?" he asked.

"Yes. I saw her before I linked up with Vancha. She's well. They settled in New York in the end. They have three children, and a fourth on the way."

"Does she still…?" Larten stopped and blushed. He had been about to ask if she still blamed him for Alicia's death, but he dreaded the answer.

"She wants to see you," Gavner said quietly. "I don't think she knows what she plans to say, but she's waiting for you to visit."

"I will, one night," Larten said. "But it is too soon."

"Be careful," Gavner warned him. "She's human. They don't last as long as us. If you wait, you might miss your opportunity."

Larten smiled thinly. "You are a wise and venerable vampire."

Gavner punched him, then smirked. "I visited your old home town too. I figured you wouldn't be keeping an eye on it while you were in pursuit of Randel Chayne."

"That was thoughtful of you," Larten said, surprised.

Gavner shrugged. "I know how close you feel to the people there. It wasn't far out of my way. So why not?"

In fact he had gone very far out of his way. Deep down, Gavner still yearned for the elder vampire to treat him like a son, not an assistant. He wasn't aware of his motivation, but he had returned to the town of Larten's birth to try and strengthen the links between them. If he could get closer to the people whom Larten cared about, perhaps Larten would start to care more about him.

"How were they?" Larten asked.

"Good," Gavner said. "Suffering because of the war, but no worse than anyone else." He waited for Larten to say something else, but the General was silent, thinking about the past. To cheer him up, Gavner said brightly, "What about you and Arra? When did that happen?"

"After Council."

"Will you mate for another term?"

"I doubt it. I think that I could love Arra, and maybe we will try again in the future. But this is the wrong time for us — for *me*. I cannot commit to her at the moment, so it will be for the best if I let her go. What about you? Is there any sign of a mate on the horizon?"

"I've no time for hanky-panky," Gavner sighed. "I'm studying to be a General and I'm finding it hard. A few more years on the road, then I'll head to Vampire Mountain to knuckle down and face my Trials."

"I did not know that you wished to become a General," Larten said. "I thought you would be content to remain an ordinary vampire."

"I thought so too for a long time," Gavner said. "I think the Generals should act more like police than soldiers. They should be peace-keepers, not warmongers. I'm worried that your anti-vampaneze brigade might stir things up and lead us down a dark, deadly road. But I figure the only way to have an influence on the direction of the Generals is from the inside. So I'm joining up, if the luck of the vampires is with me, to stand against the likes of Wester and – forgive me for saying so – you."

Larten felt proud, but he didn't show it. He had refused to be a father to Gavner in the past and he wasn't about to start showering him with paternal affection now. He didn't feel that he had a right to hail the young man as a son, given he had killed both of Gavner's parents.

"Have you learnt much from Vancha?" Larten asked.

"Not as much as I'd hoped," Gavner scowled. "A lot about hand-to-hand combat and shurikens, but not much else."

"Vancha is an excellent Prince, but a mediocre master," Larten said. "Perhaps you should spend some time with Kurda Smahlt."

Gavner frowned. "He's not much older than me."

"Age is not everything," Larten noted.

"I'll consider it," Gavner said. "At least I wouldn't have to watch him playing with his hair all the time."

"What do you mean?" Larten asked.

Gavner grinned. "Don't you know why Vancha's hair is green?"

Larten shook his head. "I assumed he dyed it."

Gavner chortled. "Don't tell him I told you, but Vancha is *very* phlegmy. He spits regularly and has to blow his nose a lot. Rather than use a handkerchief, he snorts snot into his palm. Then, instead of wiping it on the ground, he..." Gavner started to laugh.

"What?" Larten asked, laughing too in anticipation of the answer.

"He wipes his hand through his hair!" Gavner

panted. "And that's the colour your hair turns if you wipe snot through it for decades on end."

The pair of vampires laughed for a long time. They would be close to stopping, then catch each other's eye and burst into fresh gales of laughter again.

When they finally stopped giggling, Larten wiped happy tears from his cheeks and beamed at Gavner. "I lied earlier," he said. "I *have* missed you." And that was the closest he ever came to acknowledging his fondness for the young vampire who, in another time and place, could and should have been his beloved son.

CHAPTER SIXTEEN

The wedding took place the next night. Larten still didn't know who was getting married. He assumed it was a couple from one of the small villages scattered around the monastery. But nobody followed them as the vampires, Laurence and three other monks made their way to the cove, and nobody was waiting when they got there.

It was a clear, bright night, the moon close to full. Larten had washed his clothes ahead of the ceremony and was looking his best in his blood-red trousers, shirt and cape. Arra kept close to him, smiling when his back was turned, admiring the tall vampire and wishing they could spend longer together. She knew they'd part when their term elapsed, but she would have stayed with him for as long as he'd asked if she thought he truly loved her.

Vancha hadn't cleaned himself, although his hair was brushed back into less wild a shape than usual, and it gleamed in the moonlight. Larten figured the Prince must have used a few fistfuls of snot to perfect the shiny effect. Thinking about that, he giggled uncharacteristically.

Vancha frowned. "What are you laughing at?"

"Nothing, Sire," Larten replied respectfully.

The Prince squinted at him suspiciously, then faced the calm sea, studied the waves and tapped his foot impatiently. "Those Skelks have no idea of time."

"What are Skelks?" Arra asked.

"You'll find out soon," he answered.

Larten and Arra shared a bemused look, then waited quietly with the others. After a while the monks began to chant. They moved apart and stood facing the sea, heads bowed, murmuring strange rhymes. Larten scoured the horizon for boats or rafts but nothing moved on the still surface.

"There!" Arra suddenly gasped and pointed to their left.

Larten saw a large tail-fin sticking out of the water. "A dolphin?" he muttered.

"No," Arra said. "There was a face. It looked human."

Larten stared at her, wondering if she'd been drinking. But then two more fins appeared and Larten caught a glimpse of hairy but human-like faces. Soon the sheltered water of the cove was dotted with fins as a school of mysterious sea-creatures drew closer. Larten tried to count them. At least thirty of the beasts were advancing. Larten would have been worried any other time, but by the way Vancha and Kurda were smiling, he knew these must be the Skelks.

When they reached the shore, the Skelks rose to full height. They were shaped like very hairy humans from the waist up, except long, thick strands of hair linked their arms to their sides and operated like fins. Below the waist they seemed to have one long leg or tail, enshrouded by hair. But as an astonished Larten watched with disbelief, the hairs retracted into their skin and he saw that each of them had two ordinary legs beneath the covering.

The first Skelk stepped from the water. It was a man. His hair continued to retract as he limped across the sand. Strands whipped around him like snakes, then vanished into his skin. By the time he reached them, he looked like a normal human. He didn't even have a beard.

The man barked something at the monks. It sounded like the noise seals made. Larten could make no sense of the words, but Laurence obviously understood because he smiled and said, "It is a pleasure, as always."

Vancha stepped forward and made a few strange noises. They didn't sound quite the same as the sounds the man from the sea had made, but the Skelk barked in return and hugged the Prince. As they hugged, hairs shot from the man's legs, twisted around Vancha's feet, then hoisted him into the air. Seconds later he was hanging upside down, swinging from side to side, a helpless but amused captive. Vancha playfully struck at the man, who made an odd laughing sound before releasing the green-haired vampire.

Larten thought it was a strange way for a Prince to behave, but he said nothing and studied the rest of the Skelks as they crept across the sand, not looking as comfortable as they had in the water. They were a mix of men and women, with a couple of children straggling along at the rear. The women were all beautiful. They were also totally naked, like the men, and Larten felt himself blushing, especially when Arra dug an elbow into his ribs and snapped, "Avert your gaze!"

"I could say the same thing to you," Larten muttered, nodding at a few of the men who had clearly attracted Arra's attention.

"I studied anatomy when I was Evanna's assistant," she said coolly. "My interest is purely professional." But her smirk betrayed her, and Larten knew she was as mesmerised by these amazing creatures as he was.

One of the Skelks remained at the water's edge as the others advanced. This one looked different. She was shorter and her hair wasn't as luxurious. Larten found his eye drawn to her. There was something oddly familiar about the woman...

"If that's my ex-assistant, Arra Sails, she's in trouble!" the lady in the water shouted.

Arra's face dropped with shock and fear, but Larten's lit up with delight. So did Vancha's and the pair set off down the beach, whooping with excitement like a couple of boys, roaring Evanna's name as the hairs around her head parted and the ugly witch's beaming face was revealed.

"What are you doing here?" Vancha yelled, grabbing her and twirling her round. Unlike the Skelks, Evanna wasn't naked, but clad in the layers of ropes that she usually wore. Larten noted that they weren't wet, even though she'd just got out of the water.

"Why shouldn't I come, my darling little Vancha?" Evanna retorted, pinching the Prince's cheek. "Wasn't I the one who introduced you to these charming folk? They were my friends long before they were yours."

Vancha grinned and set her down. "It's a thrill to see you again, Lady. You're as gorgeous and graceful as ever."

"Shut up, fool," Evanna laughed, then offered Larten her hand, which he kissed while kneeling. "You could learn a few manners from this one," Evanna purred.

"I'm as finely mannered as any man," Vancha protested, spitting at a nearby crab and striking the top of its shell in the centre.

"Come," Evanna said, taking Vancha and Larten's hands. "We can talk later. I've been looking forward to this wedding for a long time. Let's not keep the Skelks waiting."

With that she let the vampires escort her across the beach to where the naked Skelks were gathering around the monks. Larten thought the quiet men of prayer might be embarrassed by the nudity, but they took no more notice of the Skelks than they would have of any creature in its natural form. Without batting an eyelid they went on chanting and patiently waited for everyone to settle into place, so that Laurence could begin.

It was a strange ceremony. Laurence spoke in the tongue of the Skelks, and although he couldn't mimic their sounds exactly, the sea folk listened attentively. Throughout the service, the bride and groom kept letting their hair grow, entwine with each other's, then unwind and retract again.

Vancha translated the ceremony for the other vampires and explained how the Skelks were using their hair to declare their love for one another. "The movements matter as much as the words. The Skelks don't have a huge vocabulary, since they can communicate fluently with their hair.

"The groom's name is Velap," he went on, as the pair faced each other and smiled. "The bride is Truska." He coughed and flushed slightly.

"An old girlfriend, Sire?" Larten asked.

"We spent some time together many years ago," Vancha grunted. "I think my good looks put her off in the end — she knew she couldn't keep hold of a man so desirable to women."

"Perhaps you were too modest for her," Evanna remarked drily.

"Maybe," Vancha said, nodding thoughtfully.

"How come I've never heard of Skelks before?" Gavner asked.

"They keep to themselves," Vancha said. "They're an ancient race and they can live longer than us — Truska's four hundred years old, yet still a young woman by their standards. But there aren't many of them. Certain sailors think they're evil and hunt them. They've inspired the legends of mermaids, and the more clued-in Scottish know them as Skelkies, but for the most part they mix with humans even less than we do."

Vancha lowered his voice. "I must ask you not to discuss this with anyone. They don't like it when we gossip about them."

The vampires swore themselves to secrecy, then observed the rest of the charming ceremony. The Skelks applauded when Truska and Velap finished declaring their love. Several grew beards and wound their hair together into a bed. The married couple leapt onto the mattress of hair, then were carried back to the water, where they dived in and weren't seen again.

"That's it," Laurence said, waving after the other Skelks as they swam off.

"No goodbyes?" Gavner asked.

"The Skelks don't even have a word for goodbye," Vancha said. "They think friends always meet again, if not in this life, then in another incarnation." He looked around for Evanna. She had followed the sea-creatures to the water, but had not leapt in after them. "Are you staying or going, Lady?" he called.

"Staying," Evanna replied gloomily.

"Why so sad?" Larten asked.

Evanna sighed. "I caught a glimpse of their future. They'll face hard times. The first few years will be blissful, but later..."

"We all come unstuck *later*," Vancha huffed. "I won't have dark talk tonight. Come and dance with me, Lady of the Wilds, and let the future deal with its own problems."

"Wise words, little Vancha," Evanna chuckled,

turning away from the sea. "But perhaps the monks will object."

"Not us," Laurence smiled. "We don't get to wed a pair of Skelks very often — that was only the third marriage this century. We don't drink or smoke, but most of us play instruments, virtually all of us can sing, and every one of us can dance until the sun comes up."

"The last one to the monastery is a rotten egg!" Gavner yelled, then grinned sheepishly as the others stared at him. "It's something I heard a human say."

"I think *you've* got rotten eggs instead of a brain," Vancha rumbled, then winked at the younger vampire, slapped his back and raced ahead of him.

Kurda and Arra set off after the pair, and even the monks tried to catch up with them, but Larten and Evanna held back. They smiled at each other and Evanna stroked the vampire's scar, which she had marked him with many years ago when he was young and foolish.

"I was sorry to hear about your loss," Evanna said quietly.

"Thank you." It didn't surprise Larten that she knew about Alicia. Like her father, Desmond Tiny, the witch had extraordinary supernatural powers.

"How are you progressing in your quest for revenge?" Evanna asked. She phrased it neutrally, but Larten knew immediately that she didn't approve.

"Poorly," he said. "I do not think that my prey is still alive. You could probably tell me if he was dead..."

"I could," Evanna said. "But you know that I won't."

Larten nodded. "It is not your place to get involved in such affairs. You have told me that before. Forgive me for asking."

"I hope you've been taking good care of Arra." Evanna smirked. "I don't think her knees have stopped shaking since she saw me crawl out of the sea."

"She fears that you might ask her to become your assistant again," Larten said.

"Never," Evanna snorted. "Arra wasn't cut out for that, any more than Malora was. They both belonged to the vampire world, for better or worse."

"It is a good world to belong to," Larten said, then sighed.

"You're not suffering *another* crisis of confidence, are you?" Evanna barked. "I thought you'd come to terms with the vampire life."

"I have," Larten said. "I am content to be a General. But others think I can be more, that I will become a Prince. I am not sure if I desire such power. I look at these monks and the simple lives they lead and wonder if such a quiet existence is what I secretly crave."

Evanna blinked. "You want to become a *monk*?"

"No. But there are others who work for them..."

The pair set off towards the monastery. They walked in silence until Evanna stopped abruptly. "I won't tell you what to do," she said. "But you should be true to yourself. We must all face our destiny openly. Don't turn away from it just because you have doubts. If you don't want to be a Prince, simply reject the offer if they make it."

"I cannot," Larten sighed. "It would be an honour to lead. If I am asked, I will accept and do my best for the clan. But I am afraid of where I might lead them."

"You mean into war with the vampaneze." Evanna's expression was grave.

"I believe that war is the only way to guarantee our security," Larten said. "But at the same time it would result in bitterness, suffering and death. The thought of being responsible for so much upheaval and pain..."

"You must do what your heart tells you," Evanna said softly. "The only advice I can give is to be certain of your beliefs. I detect shades of both Seba and Wester in your voice. Seba always felt he would abuse power if it was his, so he shunned it. Wester has always hated the vampaneze and plotted their downfall.

"I love and respect Seba, and I admire Wester in many ways too, but you can be a better vampire than either of them. If you are true to yourself and choose your own path, you can be a vampire of *great* standing."

Evanna started to say more, then stopped. There were limits to what she could tell a mortal. She didn't dare test those limits for fear of retribution.

Larten thought hard about what she had told him. Finally he scowled and said, "Joining the monks would be foolishness?"

"I think so," Evanna said, feeling it was safe to speak now that he had put the idea behind him. "They would welcome you and do what they could to help you adjust, but this is too withdrawn a life for one of your potential. You need to play an active role in the affairs of the night."

"Then I will continue searching for Randel Chayne," Larten said and Evanna's heart sank. Larten noted her face drop and he frowned. "Is that a mistake, Lady?"

"Of course not," she said quickly. "Don't mind me. I was thinking of something else. Come, take my hand and let's see what you're like on the dance floor."

She laughed, but her heart wasn't in it. Because Evanna had seen into Larten's future. She tried never to look at what destiny held in store for those she was fond of, but sometimes she couldn't help herself. Larten's decision would lead him into a bleak, lonely place of heartbreak and loss. If he had turned his back on revenge and war, he could have become a Prince of wisdom, sympathy and strength. He might even have saved the clan from the torments of her father, who was ruthlessly scheming against them.

But now that Larten had ignored his chance to switch courses, he was destined to play into the hands of Desmond Tiny. As a result, his future would be darker and bloodier than any he had yet to imagine.

Evanna wanted to weep for her friend and all of the others who would suffer. But instead she put on a brave face, pretended to know nothing of what lay in store for Larten and those close to him, and danced.

PART FOUR

"I saw my mother's killer tonight"

CHAPTER SEVENTEEN

New York in the late 1960s was arguably the most exciting city in the world. It was a time of great change and freedom. People were expressing themselves in fresh, forthright ways, demanding more of their leaders, redefining their culture. The young dressed in colourful, fanciful clothes. The air was alive with fast, thumping, revolutionary music. The Big Apple had always been a hectic metropolis, but now it was more vibrant and energising than ever.

Larten wasn't sure what to make of the new world as he crept across the city late at night. He was glad that the humans had put the destruction and hardships of the war behind them so quickly. But the new music was *loud*. The clothes were ungainly. And the freedoms the youth sought were far removed from those which a vampire considered appropriate.

Perhaps I am just too old to appreciate this generation, he mused to himself as he hid in the shadows of an alley and observed a group of laughing, bellowing boys and girls mill past. *They are no wilder than I was as a Cub. Gavner is right — I am turning into a stuffy old bat.* He chuckled to himself. *But I like being stuffy!*

As the group spilled out of the alley, another jostled into it. Larten decided he wouldn't get far very quickly on the ground, so he took to the rooftops, using his hardened nails to scale the walls. It wasn't as easy to dart across the roofs as it had once been. Humans stayed up later than in the past, and the city was much more brightly lit than it had been when he'd first started to explore the night. But Larten was quick and experienced, so he was able to slip across the skyline undetected.

He had visited a lot of the great cities over the past twenty years. His search for Randel Chayne had taken him all over the world. He'd concentrated on the places mentioned by Holly-Jane Galinec to begin with, and spent several years in Europe. But with no sign of the vampaneze, he drifted further afield, following trails which were sometimes decades old.

He found a vampaneze in Budapest who had known Randel and heard a rumour that he'd been seen in Korea. Seoul revealed no trace of him, but Larten ran into a vampire called Hughie who said that several vampaneze had based themselves in Australia and that the massive country was attracting more of them all the time.

Hughie had grimaced. "They like the taste of Australian blood. Personally I think it's sour, but the vampaneze go crazy for it. You might find him there."

Larten hit the major coastal cities and explored much of the rest of the country, since some of the vampaneze preferred the less densely inhabited areas. He crossed paths with six vampaneze during his time Down Under, and challenged and killed them all. But although a couple had known Randel Chayne, none had seen him recently. One swore, as he lay dying, that the killer was alive and that he knew where Randel was, but Larten thought that the vampaneze was only taunting him. It was unusual for one of their clan to lie, but imminent death could warp the tongue of even the strongest willed person.

The General's reputation had grown tenfold by the time he left Australia. Word had spread among vampires and vampaneze around the globe. The rumour was that a single vampire had driven the purple-skinned bloodsuckers from the continent, claimed it for himself and vowed to kill any vampaneze who set foot there. The children of both families of the night were impressed by the thought of a lone man defending an entire country, and those who knew the vampire's

identity spoke of him in glowing terms. By the time
Wester heard the tales, Larten had allegedly killed
thirty vampaneze and bathed in their blood for extra
strength.

Many vampaneze set sail for Australia, to face the
arrogant foe who had laid down a challenge to their
clan. If Larten had known, he would have lingered and
waited for his enemies to find him. But, having decided
that Randel wasn't present, he had already left en route
to South America by the time the first of the vampaneze
arrived.

Larten found three vampaneze in Peru. They had
formed a pack and were hunting together. He fought
all three at the same time. It was a ferocious battle
and he was seriously injured, but at the end of it he
was standing and the vampaneze lay dead at his feet.
His reputation received another boost, but the victory
brought him no nearer to finding the elusive Randel
Chayne.

Larten was aware of what was being said about him.
Wester stayed in touch and sent envoys to give him
news of what was happening at Vampire Mountain. But
he steered clear of their spiritual homeland and had
little to do with the rest of the clan. He let Wester use
his name to gather support for war with the vampaneze,
but did nothing to promote his claims to becoming a

Prince. He even avoided Council, not wishing to be distracted from his quest.

He first made his way to New York, after an absence of many decades, in the early 1960s. He had been working his way north and east, through the bustling cities of the United States, and it was an obvious place to target. But he went for another reason too — Sylva.

Larten had met with Gavner a couple of times since the monastery. The younger vampire kept urging him to visit New York and make his peace with Alicia's daughter. The guilt-stricken General had put it off as long as he could, but finally he decided to face her and let her say whatever she must. He asked Gavner to warn her that he was coming, then met her in a graveyard – the venue was her choice – late one wintry night.

"You haven't changed much," Sylva had noted bitterly as the wind whipped a scarf around her face.

"Thirty years is not a long time for a vampire," Larten had replied quietly.

"It's a lifetime for many humans," Sylva had said and hobbled forward – she'd had a lot of problems with the veins in her legs – to stand in front of him. "Do you still think about my mother?"

"Almost every night," Larten had answered truthfully.

"We don't discuss it much when he comes, but Gavner told me you're hunting the one who killed her."

"Yes," Larten had said.

"You know who it was?"

"Aye."

"Then I don't need to give you a description?"

"No."

"Good." She'd sighed. "I hate talking about it, so I won't. But I still see his face every time I fall asleep. If you find and kill him, will you inform me?"

"Of course."

They had wandered through the graveyard. After a while Sylva leant on Larten for support and they'd spoken of the old nights, the Paris they had known, Gavner, Alicia. Larten told her stories of life before Sylva was born, the early aeroplane he had flown in, Alicia's love of art, the portrait they had posed for.

"I've seen that," Sylva had said. "It's in a book that Mama kept. You're lucky it was never a bestseller or people everywhere would know what you look like."

Sylva told Larten about her life since fleeing Europe, her husband, her children, the job she had with the United Nations. Gavner had already told Larten most of it, but he pretended it was news to him — he liked listening to her speak.

Eventually she broached the topic which they had been avoiding all night. "I still hate you," she'd said sadly. "I blame you for Mama's death and I always will. You dragged her into your world of darkness, and if not for that, she might still be alive.

"But I'm about the same age now that she was when she died. I know she drove you away when she was younger, then forgave you later. I know you were honest with her when you came back, that you truly loved her. I know you didn't mean for her to be hurt, that you did what you could to save her.

"Patrice – my husband – saw many disturbing things when he returned to France and fought in the War. He saw men and women commit terrible crimes. He still sees some of those people when he travels to Europe on business. I asked him once how he can face them. He said that we can't afford to live in the past and be slaves to our memories. It's hard for him – he'll never forget or forgive – but he tries to live for the future."

At that point Sylva had stopped and taken Larten's hands. "I want to live for the future too. I want to stop hating you. You were an important part of my mother's life, and mine, and I want to feel close to you again. I don't know if I can. But I want to try. If you'll let me."

"That would please me more than anything else I

can think of," Larten had said in a strangely choked voice, and he'd held Sylva as she cried, remembering the losses of the past, hoping for a happier future.

Larten had visited her twice since then. They always met at neutral venues. Sylva refused to let him near Patrice or her children, for fear they might end up as her mother had. Larten didn't think that was likely, but he respected her wishes.

The vampire normally let Sylva choose their meeting point, but on this occasion he'd asked her to let him pick the location. Some old friends of his were going to be in the city and he wanted to introduce Sylva to them.

Sylva was waiting for him at the all-night diner where they had agreed to meet. She smiled as he entered and drew stares from the other customers, cutting an imposing figure in his red clothes and cape, with his orange hair and scar. She let him sit, then ordered for him — she was constantly trying to introduce him to new drinks. He sipped politely from the cup of coffee when it came but to be honest, he preferred the taste of bat broth.

They spoke briefly of what they had been up to since they'd last met, but Sylva couldn't contain her curiosity for long. "Where are we going?" she asked. "You were very mysterious on the phone."

"I hate telephones," Larten grumbled. "I always feel like a fool when I have to speak into one. But they have become a necessary evil. Tell me, do you enjoy the theatre?"

"Very much," she said. "But if you're going to take me to a show, I should warn you that I've seen most of the plays on Broadway."

"You will not have seen any like this," Larten assured her.

When Sylva was ready, Larten took her arm – she needed a cane to walk now – and led her to a deserted warehouse. The building was dark outside and Sylva was nervous. Then she saw other people enter and her nerves faded.

A man was waiting just inside the door. He was the tallest man she'd ever seen, and the hat he wore made him seem even taller. He had a menacing expression and very black teeth. He was glaring at them. Sylva clutched Larten's arm and got ready to defend herself with her cane if they were attacked.

"Do you have tickets?" the tall man growled.

"No," Larten said gravely. "I would not waste good money on a two-bit show like this one."

The men glowered at each other, then broke out laughing. "It's good to see you, old friend," the tall man smiled.

"Likewise," Larten said. "Sylva, this is Hibernius Tall, owner of the Cirque Du Freak."

"You run a freak show?" Sylva frowned.

"No, madam," Mr Tall said. "I run the most incredible, exciting, mindboggling freak show in the history of the world. Come, I will seat you in the front row. Any friend of Larten's is a most respected and welcome friend of mine." He glanced at the vampire and his eyes sparkled. "You may, of course, enter of your own free will."

"Very droll," Larten sighed, wishing – not for the first time – that Bram Stoker had never written that inexplicably popular book about vampires.

Sylva wasn't sure what to expect as she took her seat in front of the stage, but soon realised that Mr Tall had spoken truly. This *was* the most incredible show she'd ever seen. There was a man called Bradley Stretch who had rubbery bones — he could extend his arms and legs, tie his fingers into knots, and do a whole lot more. There was a woman who could set her eyes alight. A boy who could cut off pieces of his body and then grow them back again. And many, many more.

Sylva watched in a daze, along with the rest of the audience, as one freak after another took to the stage, each more amazing than the one before. Even Larten was surprised. The show was slicker and more wondrous than when he'd first seen it. The dancing ladies and stage magicians were relics of the past. It was now a display of pure, unique, unmatchable marvels.

Only one thing disturbed Larten. In the interval a number of small people in blue robes and hoods passed among the crowd, selling trinkets. These were the mysterious Little People, servants of Desmond Tiny. Their master had sent them to protect the cast and crew of the Cirque Du Freak during the War. Des Tiny had told Larten that he dispatched the Little People to guard the circus whenever great threats loomed on the horizon. The fact that they were still with the Cirque troubled Larten and made him wonder what sort of dangers might be lying in store.

Larten and Sylva went backstage after the show for a small party to which only a few select guests had been invited. Sylva got to meet some of the stars and chat with them about their lives, how they had been discovered by Mr Tall, what it was like to have rubbery bones or regrowable limbs.

"I think she enjoyed our little show," Mr Tall murmured to Larten, popping up beside him without warning.

"Everybody does," Larten smiled. "My

congratulations. I did not think you could improve on the old formula, but it is better than ever."

"We're constantly evolving," Mr Tall said. "Tastes are more refined than they used to be, so I can focus solely on the bizarre and freakish now. And with modern travel being what it is, I find it easier to track down fresh talent and bring new performers into the fold."

"I sometimes dream of taking to the stage again," Larten said. "But I do not think my old bag of tricks would find much favour with a modern audience."

"Don't be so sure," Mr Tall said. "We have a particularly strong line-up at the moment, but there is always room for a spot of light relief. Your sleight of hand and escape tricks are not unusual, but your speed and strength are. Naleesha – the lady who sets her eyeballs on fire – is taking a short holiday. We're playing New York for another eight nights and will be without her for the rest of our time here. We could make use of your talents."

"You are joking," Larten said sceptically.

"No," Mr Tall said. "I'm serious. Will you perform with us again?"

"I do not think–" Larten began, but Sylva had been listening and she cut in.

"Please, Larten, say you'll do it. I'd love to watch

you. If you agree to perform, I'll come every night and cheer for you until my voice breaks."

"Well," Larten chuckled, oddly nervous at the thought of stepping in front of an audience again after all these years, "with support like that, how can I refuse?" He snapped his cape and struck a pose. "Show me to my trailer, Hibernius. The real star of the show has arrived!"

CHAPTER EIGHTEEN

Larten spent most of the day rehearsing with Mr Tall. They set up a number of high-risk escapist routines. In one, Larten was locked in chains and placed beneath a door studded with sharpened stakes. The door would be held in place overhead by a rope and a member of the audience would be invited to slice through the rope with a knife. It would take them about half a minute to cut through the strands. If Larten didn't wriggle free in time, he'd be skewered in a dozen places and that would be the end of him.

Getting out of the chains wasn't the hard bit — any decent escapologist could have done that. But Mr Tall wanted it to appear as if he'd failed, so that when the stakes dropped, the audience could see him still struggling. If he darted out of harm's way at the last split-second, using his unnatural speed, he would give the impression that he'd been trapped and everyone would think he was dead.

"That should give the crowd a juicy scare," Mr Tall said enthusiastically.

The difficulty was timing it so finely that those watching wouldn't know he had escaped until after the door was raised. Larten had to do it countless times until Mr Tall was happy. It was only when one of the stakes caught the hem of his cape and nearly speared his foot that Mr Tall expressed satisfaction.

"Perfect!" he clapped. "That's what I'm after. Now let's see if we can't knock another tenth of a second off of it."

Larten would also lift several heavy weights and juggle them. Each object had spikes or sharp edges, so if he made a mistake, he'd lose a few fingers.

"I do not recall you being this bloodthirsty in the past," he complained at one point.

"Audiences are more sophisticated than before," Mr Tall said. "We have to add an authentic element of danger. They must see that the threat of injury is genuine. If you can't give them that, they will jeer you off stage."

When Larten had stretched his skills and stamina as far as he could – he was sweating through his clothes – Mr Tall dismissed him and told him to get some sleep. The General went away muttering angrily, but when the time came to perform that night – under his old nickname of Quicksilver – and he took his bows after a successful act to a chorus of cheers, he forgot about his complaints and lapped up the applause. It had been a long time since he'd been able to enjoy himself so freely, without any thoughts of his grim quest. For those brief moments he was a true part of the Cirque Du Freak again, with no other concerns in the world.

Sylva was greatly impressed and hurried backstage after the show to tell the vampire how fabulous he was. Larten tried to make light of her compliments, and the others which he was paid, but inside he was glowing. He had missed the stage life. The next week was going to be a lot of fun, and he was determined to rack up the tension another few notches by making his escapes even more life-threatening than they already were.

The next four nights passed in a happy blur. Larten slept soundly by day – Mr Tall provided him with a luxurious coffin – and practised for a couple of hours every evening. Then he relaxed and had a light meal with the other performers, before taking to the stage and burning as brightly as he could during his time in the spotlight.

Sylva came to every performance as she'd promised, and clapped and cheered louder than anyone else whenever he stepped forward to take a bow. She also came backstage after each show to congratulate him. It was the closest he had felt to her, certainly since she had been a tiny girl in Paris. The Cirque Du Freak had brought them together in a way nothing else ever had.

Later, looking back on those few delightful nights, he would curse himself for not realising that it was too good to be true, for not anticipating the sorrow and pain which always struck whenever he was happy. But at the time he genuinely had no notion that his involvement with the freakish circus would result in the deepest, cruellest cut of his long, dark, tragic life.

On the night of his sixth performance, as he was about to launch into the first of his escapes, somebody in the crowd heckled him. "Hey, ugly, get off the stage! The only freakish thing about you is your hideous face!"

Larten flushed angrily and squinted against the glare of the spotlights, scanning the crowd to find the one who had insulted him. Anger quickly gave way to delight when he spotted a grinning Gavner Purl sitting near the back. Beside him sat an even more welcome and unexpected sight — Wester Flack.

Larten was thrilled to see his old friends, regardless of the fact that Gavner continued to heckle him, and he put on an extra fine, precisely timed show. Even

Wester and Gavner had trouble keeping sight of him when he darted out of the way of the falling stakes and a massive, rolling boulder. On a couple of occasions they thought, along with the rest of the audience, that he had been squashed or speared. But the orange-haired General always reappeared to take his deserved applause.

When Larten took his final bow at the end of the show, he signalled to the pair to meet him round back. They were led through to the after-show party along with a handful of other select guests. While most of the VIPs made straight for the more remarkable stars of the show, the vampires hurried over to Larten.

"What are you doing here?" the General beamed. He was particularly surprised to see Wester.

"We're messengers of good fortune," Wester grinned, but before he could continue, a teenager stuck his head between the two vampires.

"Is this him?" the boy gasped.

"The one and only," Gavner said.

The excited teen extended a hand. "It's an honour to meet you, sir. My father told me many tales about you."

Larten shook the young man's hand, smiling uncertainly. "I am trying to place your face, but I do not know..."

"My name's Jimmy, sir. Jimmy Ovo."

It clicked. "The undertaker in Berlin!" Larten exclaimed. "Your father was helping Kurda Smahlt when I met him. He travelled with us for a while. What in the name of the gods are you doing here with these two?"

"I met James when I was with Kurda," Gavner explained. "He went back into undertaking after the war. I've kept in touch. It's handy knowing a man in his line — he and his contacts are able to provide us with bottled blood when we need it. I dropped by to see him on our way. He told me Jimmy was in New York on holiday, so I thought I might as well invite him to the Cirque Du Freak while I was here."

"I'm going to follow my old man into the family business," Jimmy said. "I'll be happy to supply you with all the blood you require once I'm established. Any time you need a top-up, just come ask."

"I will do that," Larten smiled.

Before Jimmy could start quizzing Larten about his experiences during the war, Gavner sent him to chat with some of the other performers. "He's a nice kid," Gavner said when the boy was out of earshot, "but a bit too bubbly sometimes."

"All of the young are lively," Larten said. "I remember..." He spotted Sylva and beckoned her to join them. He thought she'd be delighted to see Gavner again, and he was keen to introduce her to Wester — the pair knew much about each other, but had never actually met. But Sylva's face was pale and she shook her head when Larten waved, then turned and stumbled away, limping heavily, her hand shaking as it gripped the head of her cane. Larten was confused, but before he could follow to investigate, Wester spoke.

"We have important news," he said, his face aglow. "We came as fast as we could. We didn't want you to hear it from anyone else. Can we go somewhere private to tell you?"

"Don't be melodramatic," Gavner laughed. "Here's as good a place as any."

Wester glanced around. Nobody was paying any attention to them. He chuckled ruefully. "You're right. No point beating about the bush. Larten, you're going to become a Prince."

"Of course I am," Larten said sarcastically. "You and Gavner are here to invest me, I suppose?"

"I'm serious," Wester said and Larten's smile faded. "Paris has nominated you. Arrow and Mika have already approved the nomination. Chok Yamada and Vancha haven't yet been back to Vampire Mountain to vote, but I'm certain Vancha will recommend you. Sire

Yamada will probably reject the nomination, to ensure it goes to the vote. You know what it's like — the Princes have the power to elect a new Prince by themselves if they all agree, but they prefer to let Generals vote on the matter."

"That's *if* Chok makes it back," Gavner added gloomily. "He's in poor health according to reports. We're expecting bad news any night now."

"Even in death may he be triumphant," Larten murmured, making the death's touch sign in honour of the ageing Prince.

"It's happening," Wester said, barely able to contain his excitement. He gripped Larten's arms and squeezed. "Everything's finally falling into place."

Larten smiled crookedly. The news was hard to absorb. The Princes were the most revered of vampires. By becoming one, he was guaranteed a privileged place in the annals of the clan. Assuming the Generals supported his nomination, in a few years he would have more power than he had ever imagined. Any honourable vampire would lay down his life for Larten and obey his every command. He would be able to exert tremendous influence over thousands of vampires, maybe even persuade the other Princes to lead them into war with the vampaneze.

Larten was ecstatic yet scared. He didn't know

whether to cheer or cringe. Part of him wanted to be invested immediately, but another part wished that he could postpone the honour. He guessed that every Prince's senses reeled when they first heard of their nomination. The confusion would no doubt pass once the shock wore off.

"You did not need to come and tell me in person," Larten said.

"There's gratitude for you," Gavner huffed.

Larten shook his head. "I am delighted to see you both, but why come all this way when you could have passed the message to me by other means?"

"I need to campaign for you," Wester said. "Some Generals don't like the fact that you're associated with me. There will be opposition to your nomination. I want to gather support for you, remind the doubters of your triumphs over the vampaneze. The next few years are vital. We need to get as many Generals on our side as we can, so that you can win the vote of a clear majority."

"Will you campaign for me too?" Larten asked Gavner, smiling to show it was meant as a joke — he knew the young vampire didn't approve of his and Wester's plans to provoke a war.

"I don't think you need help," Gavner said. "In my opinion Wester's worrying for nothing. Some vampires will object to your nomination, but not many. You'll sweep in without any problems. I just happened to be in Vampire Mountain when Wester heard and I wanted to come share the good news with you."

"Speaking of which," Larten frowned, "how do you know about the nomination? It is meant to be a secret until all of the Princes have been consulted."

Wester laughed. "When did that ever happen? Word spreads swiftly through the Halls of Vampire Mountain."

"Are you sure it is not just a rumour?" Larten asked.

"Positive," Wester said. "Seba confirmed it — Paris asked him for his thoughts before nominating you. He asked me to pass on his congratulations. He said to tell you he was proud, and that he was confident you would prove an immense credit to the clan."

Larten felt tears tickling the corners of his eyes but he blinked them away before they had time to fully form. "Well," he said, stroking his scar, "this is a lot to take in. I am glad you did not tell me before my performance — if I had been distracted, I might have missed my mark and you could have been burying me tonight instead of celebrating my nomination."

The vampires laughed and clapped Larten's back. They spent the next few hours discussing the future and what lay in store for the soon-to-be Prince. Larten still had trouble believing it, and grimaced each time one of them referred to him as *Sire Crepsley*. Wester was already plotting their strategy.

"I think we can gather enough support to launch an offensive in ten, maybe fifteen years," he mused aloud. "Paris nominated you, so we can probably rely on his vote. Arrow will definitely fall in with us once he sees how passionate you are about this. Vancha and Mika will be more difficult to persuade, but if we can get most of the Generals behind us, they'll give their blessing too."

Gavner didn't like it when the pair spoke of war and wiping out the vampaneze, but he was only an ordinary General – he had passed his Trials eight years earlier – and he figured it wasn't his place to lecture them. If Wester was right and this was the wish of the clan, he would have to swallow his misgivings and fall in behind Larten as he led them all to war.

The vampires stayed up talking long after everyone else had gone home or to bed. (Jimmy Ovo had left for a party. His parting shot to a bemused Larten was, "Catch you later, orangey dude!") But finally even the creatures of the night grew tired. Larten offered his friends a place to sleep. Gavner accepted but Wester said that he had to move on.

"There are a few vampires based in and around New York," he said. "I want to track them down, find out where they stand, try to win them over if they're against your nomination. I'll be in the city another few nights and will call again to see you before I leave."

Gavner fell asleep in a hammock beside Larten's coffin, and soon he was snoring soundly. Larten couldn't sleep, and not just because of Gavner's rasping snores. He kept thinking about his investiture, how his life would change, what it would be like to go to war. Randel Chayne would no longer be able to hide. If he was alive, he'd have to fight along with the rest of his clan. One way or another, Larten's quest was drawing towards a close.

He decided to get some fresh air before the sun rose. Slipping out, he took to the streets and set off on what should have been a long, taxing walk. But he didn't get very far. Passing the all-night diner where he'd met Sylva a week earlier, he spotted her inside, hunched over a mug of coffee, tears streaming down her face.

Larten paused by the window and studied the weeping woman. She had looked upset when he saw her after the show. He'd meant to ask if she was all right, but had been distracted by Wester's news. He thought of leaving her to cry in private, but he hated seeing her like this and didn't want to abandon her without trying to help. Maybe something had happened to Patrice or one of her children.

Sylva didn't look up as he sat opposite her, but by the way her fingers tightened on her mug, he knew she was aware of his presence. He said nothing for a time, letting her recover and compose herself. Finally she met his gaze and wiped tears from her bloodshot eyes.

"I was waiting for you," she sniffed. "I couldn't go home. I'd have waited all day if I had to. I won't put Patrice's or the children's lives in danger."

Larten frowned. "What are you talking about?"

"You always said that you knew who he was," Sylva moaned. "I never described him because I didn't think I needed to. You said that you *knew*."

Larten shook his head dumbly. She wasn't making sense.

Sylva took a deep breath, then wheezed, "I saw my mother's killer tonight."

Larten froze. For a long minute he stared at the ashen woman, his thoughts in a mad whirl. Finally he placed his hands flat on the table and said dully, "Where was he? In the audience? On the roof?"

Sylva laughed sickly. "You've been a fool. The only reason I can forgive you is that I know how much this will hurt. I even considered not telling you — it would have been easier to leave you to your fantasy. But she was my mother. It's been a long time, but I still want to see her assassin pay for what he did. I can't let him go free, even to spare your feelings."

Larten frowned. "I do not understand. I hate Randel Chayne. My heart will fill with joy when I kill him."

"Such a fool," Sylva sighed. Then she laid her soft hands over Larten's and spoke gently, knowing she would destroy his world with her words, but unable to withhold the truth from him. "The killer didn't hide. He didn't need to. He would have been more careful if he knew I was at the show, but thinking that he had nothing to fear, he acted without caution.

"You have been betrayed," she whispered. "I don't know what his name is, but by the way you acted in his presence, he's clearly not the one you knew as Randel Chayne. For all these decades you've been chasing the wrong man."

And as she went on, Larten felt waves of madness surround and engulf him, claiming him for blood-drenched, heartbroken delirium once more.

CHAPTER NINETEEN

Larten spent the day in his coffin, listening to Gavner snore, thinking everything through, putting all of the pieces together. He was calmer than he should have been. If this had happened forty or fifty years ago, he would have flown into a murderous rage. But he was older now, more world-weary. This was the worst thing that had ever happened to him, but he wasn't shocked. He had seen enough in his many decades to know that this was just the way things worked. Vulnerable boys like Vur Horston were killed all the time. True-hearted girls like Malora met with sticky ends every day. Selfish, cynical men like Tanish Eul were everywhere. He had long been incapable of claiming an innocent's view of the world, so Larten could only feel sadness and shame — sad that he'd been betrayed, ashamed that he hadn't spotted the deception earlier.

He rose an hour before sunset. Gavner was still snoring. Larten considered leaving while his ex-assistant slept, but that would have been unfair. He couldn't take Gavner with him, regardless of the promise he had made to include him in the execution of Alicia's killer if they ever learnt of his whereabouts, but it would be wrong to exit without serving any sort of notice. So he bent and gently woke the sleeping General.

"Why'd you wake me so early?" Gavner yawned.

"I have to leave," Larten said. "I need you to deliver some messages for me."

"What sort of messages?"

"First, tell Hibernius that I cannot be part of the show tonight. It probably will not come as any surprise to him, but pass on my apologies anyway."

"OK." Gavner rubbed sleep from his eyes. "Who's the next message for?"

"Paris Skyle. Tell him that I do not want to become a Prince. I am sick of this business and want nothing more to do with the clan. I do not even wish to be a General any longer. Tell him I have resigned with immediate effect."

Gavner scowled. He thought Larten was joking and he was trying to figure out the punchline. Then he focused on the vampire's dark expression and realised this wasn't a gag.

"Larten!" he gasped, clambering to his feet. "What happened? Why are you saying this? What—"

"I do not care to discuss the matter," Larten interrupted. "I was once your master. I might even have been a father to you if I had not been so stuck in my *stuffy* ways." He smiled fleetingly, but it was a lonely, distressed shade of a smile. "If you bear any love for me, you will do as I request and ask no questions."

Gavner gulped then nodded slowly. He was silently cursing himself for being such a sound sleeper. He didn't know what he'd missed, but something had gone seriously amiss with the world while he slumbered.

"There is one more message," Larten said evenly. "Tell Seba that I am sorry if I disappointed him. I will always love and respect him, but he should not expect a visit from me or Wester any time soon. In fact he might never see us again."

"Wester's leaving too?" Gavner asked, blinking with confusion.

"We must both... *withdraw*," Larten said. "One of us might return to him some night in the future, but it is unlikely."

Gavner shook his head helplessly. "I don't understand."

Larten gave the young vampire's shoulder a squeeze. "There are some things in life we can never understand, things we are better off *not* understanding. Pass on my messages. Try to be a General of good standing. Make me proud of you."

With that he turned and left. Gavner didn't call after him. He had lost his voice. The last time he'd felt this bewildered and alone was when Larten and Vancha tracked him down in Petrograd and killed Tanish Eul. But he felt even worse now, as he was about to lose someone who meant much more to him than Tanish had.

Finally, when his throat cleared, he mumbled, "Goodbye... *father*."

But Larten never heard. He was already gone.

Larten was able to track Wester mentally. The pair had bonded many decades ago and one could always locate the other, no matter where in the world they were. He found Wester shortly after dusk, near the top of one of New York's many towering skyscrapers, conversing with another vampire. Larten studied them from his perch outside the window. It didn't bother him that he was high off the ground, clinging to the wall like a spider, facing certain death if his grip slipped. He felt at one with the world up here.

Wester was talking about Larten becoming a Prince, and the possibility of war with the vampaneze. He was animated, making grand promises and pledges. The other vampire looked dubious.

Larten sent a mental burst to Wester. Vampires

couldn't communicate at length in this manner, but they could exchange short messages. *I need to speak with you,* Larten transmitted. *Meet me on the roof.*

Wester paused and frowned, then carried on as if nothing had happened. After a minute he made an excuse to leave and said he would return shortly. As Wester exited, Larten crawled up the outside of the building, digging his nails into the bricks, climbing swiftly. He hauled himself onto the roof before Wester got there. When the guard arrived, Larten was standing close to the edge, staring out over the city, his back to Wester.

"What's up?" Wester asked.

"It will be a fine night," Larten replied, gazing at the clear sky.

Wester laughed uneasily. "You didn't come here to discuss the weather." He could tell something was wrong by the way Larten stood so stiffly.

"You have always been a brother to me," Larten said. "Along with Seba, you are the closest family I have had since turning my back on those who brought me into this world."

"I feel the same way about you." Wester's face twisted into a worried frown. "Is something wrong with our old master?"

"No." Larten cracked his knuckles and changed

the subject. "It is strange how Randel Chayne disappeared. Vampires and vampaneze often die in the wilds and are never discovered, but if he had been trailing me, he would have been frequenting the cities of Europe. There should have been *some* trace of him."

"I suppose he tried to hide after..." Wester cleared his throat diplomatically.

"That is what I imagined too," Larten said. "I thought, after he killed Alicia in Paris, that he fled and lay low for a while, and was either in hiding or had died in an accident at some point over the years."

Larten turned and looked at Wester calmly. "When did you kill him?"

Wester blinked, caught off guard. "What?"

"I assume you killed him before you slaughtered Alicia, so that you could be certain of being able to point the finger of blame at him. Was it days before? Weeks? Months? How long had you been planning it, Wester? How long did you have it in mind to kill the woman I loved, pin the blame on Randel Chayne, turn me against the vampaneze and use me to lead our people into war?"

Wester gulped and desperately searched for a way out of this dire predicament. But he quickly realised that nothing he said could have any impact on the stern-faced General. Larten would not have levelled such an accusation at him if he wasn't one hundred per cent sure.

"How did you find out?" Wester asked softly.

"Sylva saw you after you killed her mother, as you were fleeing. She was at the show last night and recognised you when you came backstage."

Wester sighed. "I should have killed her in Paris. When I looked back on it later, I regretted being merciful. I often meant to track her down and eliminate her, but I didn't want to hurt you any more than I already had, and as the years passed it seemed as if I had nothing to worry about. I stopped thinking of her as a potential threat."

"You are an amateur villain," Larten noted cynically.

"Aye," Wester grimaced. "Like Tanish Eul, I was never cut out for murder. Clumsy assassins like us should leave it to the professionals." He was calm now that his deception had been revealed, calmer than he had ever thought he would be when he'd imagined this scenario. And he had imagined it countless times over the years, haunted by memories of what he had done and fears of what would happen if his crime came to light. "How much do you want to know?"

"Not a lot," Larten answered curtly. "I have been able to work out most of it. When you saw that you were losing the support of the clan, you made one last attempt to convince me to join you. When that failed, you killed Alicia and framed Randel Chayne."

"Having already executed him," Wester nodded. "I'd been keeping tabs on Randel for years. I have contacts among the vampaneze who yearn for war as much as I do — we're strangely united by our hatred of each other. They kept me abreast of his movements. I killed him before I came to you, knifed him while he was asleep. An ignoble end for a child of the night, but he was an ignoble individual, so I didn't worry too much about it."

"Did Desmond Tiny put the idea in your head when he came to visit you at Vampire Mountain?" Larten asked.

"Not directly," Wester said. "He told me that I needed your support to lead the clan to war, and he mentioned the fact that if you hated the vampaneze as much as I did – if you lost someone close to them as I had – you might sympathise more with my cause. But he never mentioned Alicia specifically."

"He did not need to," Larten said. "He knew you were clever enough to put two and two together." For the first time a bitter edge crept into his voice.

"I had to do it," Wester said, staring down at his hands, remembering that awful night, the bloodstains on his fingers, sobbing uncontrollably as he took Alicia's life, hating himself, but pressing on regardless.

"*Had to?*" Larten snarled.

"The vampaneze must be eradicated," Wester said. "You were the key. That's become more obvious with every passing year. It was your destiny to lead the clan to glory, to destroy our enemies and secure our future. But sometimes destiny needs a helping hand. I didn't want to do it, but ultimately she was only one woman. What's a single life measured against the lives of everyone in our clan?"

Larten trembled with rage but said nothing, waiting for the emotion to pass. He didn't want to get into a war of words with Wester. It was too late for that. Nothing either of them said could change what had happened or what must be done now.

"It will be a fine night," Larten said again, returning to the subject of the weather.

"I suppose," Wester frowned, glancing at the sky.

"A good night to die," Larten added.

"Oh." Wester's features clouded over. "You plan to kill me?"

"We will duel," Larten said. "I am your superior in combat, as we both know, but perhaps I will make mistakes in my current unsettled state. Either way it will be a fair fight."

Wester nodded. "Will you give me an honourable burial if you win? Will you tell Seba I fell in battle and praise my name in the Halls of Vampire Mountain?"

"No," Larten croaked, tears springing to his eyes.

Wester had been waiting for the tears. As Larten blinked them away, Wester thrust forward. His fingers twisted into a hook and he lashed at Larten's stomach, hoping to slice it open and end the fight early.

Although Larten was temporarily blinded, he heard Wester close in on him and shimmied aside as the guard struck. Wester's nails cut through the material of Larten's red cloak but didn't even scratch his flesh.

Larten caught Wester's outstretched arm and twisted it up behind his back, snapping the bones in several places. Wester screamed and spun away, his arm hanging uselessly by his side, face pale with pain and shock.

Larten darted at the injured guard. Wester tried to drive him back with his good hand, but Larten caught his fist mid-air then chopped at his wrist. He had only meant to shatter the bones, but he struck harder than intended and his nails tore through Wester's flesh and severed the guard's hand.

They were close to the edge of the building. Wester watched as if in a dream as his hand bounced off the roof and fell into the abyss beyond, the fingers still twitching as they dropped upon the unsuspecting city below.

Wester staggered and almost toppled off the roof after his hand. Larten grabbed the guard and held him by the pale grey cloth of his jacket. Wester was defenceless now, unable to strike back. Blood spurted from his wrist, soaking the pair of them. The fight was over and both vampires knew it.

"I... love... you," Wester moaned pitifully.

"I love you too," Larten whispered, then dug his fingers into the soft flesh of his best friend's throat and crushed. As Wester's dying gurgles were whipped away by the wind, Larten wrapped his arms around him and howled at the sky like an agonised wolf, floods of tears streaming down his cheeks, clutching his blood-brother tightly as the warmth seeped from his limp, lifeless form.

PART FIVE

"this was his destiny"

CHAPTER TWENTY

Larten buried Wester in a field far beyond the borders of New York, having flitted for a couple of hours, the corpse slung across his shoulders. He said no words of mourning and put up no marker, just dug a hole, laid Wester into it and filled it in again. He stood over the grave for a long time, head bowed. He wasn't crying now but he felt hollow inside. Finally, without warning, he turned and jogged away. Soon he was running, and then he flitted, leaving Wester to cool and rot in the earth behind.

He never returned to the grave in the years to come, but in his dreams he went back often.

Larten knew where he was headed even before he consciously decided on his path. The future gaped ahead of him like an ugly, open wound. He had no idea what he would do once he recovered from this terrible night, if he'd ever return to the clan, if he'd even find the strength to carry on living. But he knew the perfect place to hole-up while he tried to deal with his shock.

Larten had wandered the globe idly in the past when he'd felt lost, but now he had a place where he would be welcomed, where the outside world could not intrude. He would never be able to call the place home, and he knew he must move on in the end, but for the next few months, or years, or however long it took, he could rest there and suffer silently within the peace and quiet of the crumbling monastery walls.

Laurence was waiting for Larten when he returned from his night's activities. The monk was an old man now and he didn't sleep much. He often sat with Larten late at night when the vampire had finished his chores. The men rarely spoke, just enjoyed the darkness and the silence, the sense of being all alone in the world yet connected to something bigger than either of them.

Larten had been digging a ditch. It was work which the monks could have done but he liked to keep busy, so they were always looking for jobs for him. He had pushed himself hard, as he did most nights, and was sweating through the dark clothes which he had worn since coming to volunteer at the monastery. He hadn't shaved in the last decade and his beard was long and thick, flecked in a couple of places with grey streaks, at odds with his head of orange hair.

Laurence was seated outside the monastery walls. There was a chair to his left and a small cage on the ground to his right. He nodded pleasantly at Larten as the vampire sat beside him.

The pair studied the countryside in comfortable silence. It was a clear night but there was a chill in the air. Winter would be upon them soon and the sea would rage with storms. The Skelks had already moved on ahead of the changing season and it would be spring before they returned. Laurence hoped that he would be alive to welcome them back, but he was an old man and he took nothing for granted.

"I love the smell of salt water," Laurence commented. "We live so close to the sea, it's in the air all the time, so I often forget how much I cherish it. Every once in a while I make myself stop, clear my nostrils and breathe in deeply."

"I like it too," Larten said. "It brings back sad memories sometimes but I enjoy it regardless."

Laurence nodded understandingly. Larten had told him about the ship, when he'd killed all those people. He had told the monk everything over the course of the past ten years. He hadn't meant to confess when he came. For many months he said nothing to anybody, merely worked silently and slept. But eventually he found himself confiding in the patient, kindly monk. As their friendship strengthened, he gradually unburdened more of his secrets and sins until he had nothing left to hide.

Laurence never passed judgement on Larten or recommended ways in which he might atone for his crimes. The vampire didn't want advice, just company, and Laurence was pleased to offer that without any strings attached. He didn't even pray on Larten's behalf, as the vampire would have considered that deceitful. He had learnt a lot about the clan during their talks, and while he didn't think he would ever understand vampires fully, he knew they were creatures of great honesty and respected those who valued the truth as much as they did.

"This is a night for Madam Octa," Laurence said, reaching for the cage by his feet. A huge, multi-coloured spider was crouched in the centre of the cage on long, hairy legs, a green, purple and red ball of unconcealed menace. Laurence had been given the spider by one of his visitors a couple of years earlier. The woman had come to visit the Skelks and the gift was her way of thanking the monk for looking after her.

A tin whistle — Laurence referred to it as a flute

– hung from the side of the cage. Laurence handed it to Larten. The monk had taught him how to use it and Larten now played a tune as Laurence unlatched the cage and took out Madam Octa. He petted her as she rested in the palm of his hand, then nodded at Larten. The monk couldn't control the spider but Larten had a special way with animals. At his gentle mental bidding, Madam Octa crawled up Laurence's arm and over his face. She spun cobwebs across his eyes and scratched his nose. She tickled his lips until he smiled, then wove a web around one of his teeth and pulled on it as if she was a dentist trying to remove a rotten molar.

The pair continued in this fashion for an hour, playing with the spider like a couple of schoolboys. They never grew tired of her, and although they repeated familiar tricks most nights, they always experienced the same sense of delight as when she had first performed for them.

Laurence was sad when he returned Madam Octa to his cage. He would miss her when she was gone.

"Have you enjoyed your time with us?" he asked Larten.

"Yes," Larten said, surprised by the question.

"The years have passed quickly, haven't they?"

"They usually do," Larten muttered.

"How many more decades do you think you will see?"

Larten shrugged. "I never like to tempt fate."

"But if you stay in good health and avoid accidents?" Laurence pressed.

"I could live another three or four hundred years," Larten said. "A few more if the luck of the vampires is with me."

Laurence sighed. "I would love to see the world three hundred years from now. You are a fortunate man."

"It is not too late for you to be blooded," Larten joked.

Laurence smiled. "I am satisfied with the time that I have been given. It would be nice to live longer, but I won't ask for more years than the Maker has seen fit to grant me."

"A pity," Larten said. "You would have made a good vampire."

The men shared a laugh, then Laurence said casually, "Where will you go when you leave us?"

Larten frowned. "That is a strange question. Do you wish to be rid of me?"

"You know that I don't," Laurence said. "But I think *you* want to go."

Larten gaped at the monk. "How did you know?

I have been thinking of it, but I had not made up my mind or spoken of it with anyone."

"I haven't lived as long as you, my friend, but I'm old for a human and I like to believe I've learnt a bit in my time. Your gaze has been wandering inland for many months now. Our life is not for you any longer."

Larten nodded. "I wish it was, but you speak truly. I have felt restless lately."

"Good!" Laurence beamed.

"You *do* want to get rid of me," Larten accused him.

Laurence shook his head. "I only mean it's good that you feel it is time to move forward. This was never the life for you. It was a temporary retreat. You needed us while you were confused and lost. We gave you shelter and support, so that you could recover. The fact that you wish to resume your life is a sign that you are over the worst. For that I give thanks."

"I will never truly be over it," Larten said softly.

"No," Laurence said. "Nor should a man forget such a terrible thing. But if you'll forgive an old monk for preaching, we can't fester in purgatory forever. You need to move on and I'm delighted that you finally feel that you can."

"I have wanted to leave for almost a year," Larten

confessed. "But I am afraid. The world beyond has always hurt me and I fear being hurt again."

"The world hurts us all in one way or another," Laurence said, "but we can hurt ourselves too. If you follow your destiny, you stand a chance of knowing true happiness. If you hide from it, you will never be content."

Larten took a deep breath and let it out slowly. "I meant to stay for the winter – there is much to be done when the weather is bad – but perhaps I will reconsider and go before the frost sets in."

"There's no rush," Laurence said. "But if you feel you must leave, don't worry about us. We will struggle on without you." He patted the top of the cage. "I want you to take Madam Octa when you go."

"No," Larten protested. "She is yours. I know how much you enjoy her."

"You're wrong," Laurence said. "I enjoy watching *you* play with her. We have no personal possessions here. I never thought of her as belonging to me. Besides, I can't control her the way you do. I will be happier thinking of you teaching her new tricks and showing her to people in distant countries."

"If you are sure…" Larten said.

"I am." Laurence stood and stretched. He sniffed the wind blowing in off the sea. "It will be a harsh winter, I think." He glanced at Larten and smiled. "But we will relish the change. And no matter what the world throws at us, I am sure that we will face it unafraid, and thrive in our own strange, individual ways."

CHAPTER
TWENTY-ONE

Larten had no idea what the future might ultimately hold in store for him. But in the short-term he knew exactly what he wanted to do. As soon as he left the monastery, he set off in search of the Cirque Du Freak.

Mr Tall had been expecting him, and Larten wasn't surprised to find that he had already adjusted the running order to slot in the vampire.

"What does it say?" Larten asked when Mr Tall handed him a flier listing all of the performers who would be taking part in the next show.

"*Larten Crepsley and his performing spider — Madam Octa!*"

Larten frowned. "You want me to perform with my pet?"

"Your escape routines are fun," Mr Tall said, "but Madam Octa will excite the crowd. Most people are afraid of spiders. When they see one as large and deadly as her, crawling over your face..." He chuckled sadistically.

"Why use my real name?" Larten asked. "I prefer Quicksilver."

"Quicksilver is a good name for an escape artist," Mr Tall agreed. "But I want you to present a serious, solemn face to the world. *Larten Crepsley* sounds more mysterious and commanding."

Larten shrugged. "As you please."

Mr Tall smiled, then told Larten to go practise. "You start tomorrow night and I want you to hit the ground running. Forget about the soft life of Vampire Mountain — here, you'll have to work hard for your living!"

The years since *had* been hard, but enjoyable too. It had taken Larten a while to adapt to his new routine but now he loved performing onstage with Madam Octa. He felt like he was a true part of the Cirque Du Freak when he had the incredible spider with him, a unique performer like the rest of the cast.

He avoided contact with other vampires while they were travelling, but he did visit Sylva to tell her that her mother's killer had been executed. Sylva was frail and sickly when he found her. She wasn't glad to see him, and when he was getting ready to leave, she asked him not to visit her again.

"I'm not long for this world," she sighed, "and I want my last few years to be peaceful. I don't blame you for what happened, but every time I see you, I remember, and I'm at a point in my life where I'd rather try to forget."

Larten honoured her wishes and never enquired after Sylva again, though he thought of her often, recalling the evenings when he, Gavner, Alicia and the girl would stroll through the park like any ordinary, happy family.

Larten also met Jimmy Ovo a few times. The teenager had matured and abandoned his original plan to become a mortician like his father. But he hadn't strayed too far from the family business — he'd trained as a pathologist, so he still spent most of his time dealing with corpses.

Larten liked dropping in on Jimmy if the Cirque Du Freak passed near his home, to stock up on bottled blood, but also for news of the clan. Gavner had kept in touch with Jimmy and Larten was keen to keep abreast of the young General's doings. Although he would never allow himself to think of Gavner as a son, he liked to keep tabs on what the good-hearted vampire was up to. He rested easier when he knew that Gavner was safe and content, making his way in the world.

His only meeting with another vampire came several

years after he'd linked up with the Cirque Du Freak. He was practising with Madam Octa one night, a few hours before the latest show was due to start, when he spotted the unmistakable figure of Vancha March stumbling into camp. Vancha had a distressed, shivering woman with him. She was wrapped in furs and weeping. As they passed, Larten realised it was the Skelk he'd seen get married, the woman called Truska.

Mr Tall didn't appear for the show that night and Larten – as he'd done a few times before – took the owner's place and introduced the acts. He wrestled with and subdued the Wolf Man when the beast broke free. The Wolf Man couldn't be controlled, but he could be influenced by Mr Tall, who had taught him never to kill when he went wild at the start of a show, merely to bite off a hand or foot. The circus master had a bag of magical powder which could be used to reattach severed limbs. Larten thought it was a tad extreme – he felt sorry for the people who were attacked – but Mr Tall said it was the perfect way to start the show, and in matters such as these he was rarely wrong.

Larten's job was easier after he'd dealt with the Wolf Man. The rest of the show passed smoothly, though he couldn't help wondering about Vancha and Truska. He thought about slipping away at the end to avoid the Prince, but that would have been an insult to their esteemed visitor.

Vancha tracked down Larten close to dawn, as the vampire was getting ready for sleep. He grunted a greeting and perched on the end of the ex-General's coffin. He studied Larten silently, then mumbled, "I suppose you had a good reason for snubbing the will of the Princes and turning your back on the clan?"

"Aye," Larten said quietly.

"Can you tell me what it was?"

"No."

Vancha nodded. "As you wish."

"What happened to Truska?" Larten asked.

"Her husband and daughter were killed by fishermen." Vancha sighed. "When a Skelk is widowed, she has to live in mourning, apart from the others, for twenty or thirty years. I offered her a home at the Cirque Du Freak. I knew Hibernius would take her in."

"That was kind of you," Larten noted.

Vancha shrugged. "It was no more than I'd do for any friend. No more than I'd do for *you*."

Larten smiled gratefully at the confirmation that the Prince still considered him a friend.

Vancha burped loudly, then said, "I'd like to stay but I have to crack on. We can't all flee our responsibilities and live the high life."

Chapter Twenty-one

"Very droll," Larten grimaced, pleased to be teased.

Vancha headed for the door, then hesitated. "Nobody's seen Wester since you told Gavner that you were sick of us all."

Larten's expression never changed. "Is that so?"

"There have been all sorts of rumours," Vancha went on. "The anti-vampaneze brigade has split and there's been no talk of war recently. Kurda's even convinced a lot of Generals that the time is right to push for a reunion. We might see true peace between the clans in our lifetime if he gets his way."

"That would be a good thing," Larten said.

"You don't hate the vampaneze any more?" Vancha asked.

"No," Larten said. "Life is too short for hate."

"You sound like you might be learning something at last," Vancha snorted. "Do you want me to give your regards to Seba, maybe pass on news about Wester?"

"Tell him…" Larten gulped, then lowered his voice. "Tell him I do not know any vampire of that name."

Vancha blinked with surprise, then spat sadly. He was terribly curious but he knew that Larten would never tell anyone what had happened. He nodded gruffly, then set off to reluctantly deliver the message to Seba Nile. As little as Larten had said, it would tell the elderly quartermaster all that he needed to know about the fate of his ex-assistant, and more than he'd ever wished to hear.

A couple of years later, Larten clung to a wall high above the stage and waited patiently. They had just completed a show in a town like any other, having performed in an old, abandoned cinema theatre. It had all gone smoothly, as usual, but Larten had a feeling this was no ordinary night, that his life was about to change in some momentous way. Whether it would be for the better or the worse, he could not say.

The vampire was used to people gasping and cringing when he came onstage with Madam Octa — the spider sent shivers of fear down the stiffest of spines. But tonight a boy had gasped in an unusual fashion. It hadn't been a gasp of fear but of recognition.

As he'd performed, Larten had carefully scanned the crowd and located the boy. He was sitting near the front with a friend. The other youth was fascinated by Madam Octa, as most people were, but the boy who'd gasped only had eyes for the orange-haired handler. He followed Larten's every movement, captivated, nervous, yet also strangely eager.

There was no after-show party that night. Larten had meant to go feed, but instead he returned to the stage and climbed the wall to hide in the shadows near the top of the building. After a while he heard noises from the balcony opposite his perch. With his sharp eyesight, he spotted the second boy – the friend – edging forward. The boy was terrified but he pushed on. A foolish but brave lad by the look of him.

Several minutes later, the boy who had gasped wandered onto the stage. Larten studied him intently. For some reason he felt excited yet tense. He had existed in a safe, quiet place for the last few years, content to drift along at the Cirque Du Freak. But he'd always known the time would come to put the circus world behind him and face the future with purpose, and his instinct was telling him that these boys would be the catalyst for that.

The vampire considered keeping to the shadows and rejecting the call of fate. His life would probably be a lot simpler if he clung to the wall and slipped out of town as soon as the boys drifted away from the theatre. Hurt and pain might swoop down to claim him again if he got involved with this pair.

But Larten was through running from the challenges of life. He wasn't afraid of the future or the prospect of death. As he hung in the darkness, he had a sense of the universe clicking into place around him, of being in the right spot at the right time. No matter where he went from here, no matter what happened from this night onwards, this was his destiny. And it was a relief, after all this time and so many setbacks, not to be afraid of whatever life held in store.

With a gesture of both acceptance and defiance, the vampire let go of the wall. Spreading his arms, letting his cloak billow out behind him, he dropped towards the stage like a bat. In the balcony, the young boy toppled backwards with fright, then shakily rose to his knees and stared at the man standing over his cowering friend. In his flamboyant red clothes, with his unnatural orange hair, pale skin, jagged scar and penetrating gaze, there could be no mistaking him.

Mr Crepsley!

THE SAGA OF LARTEN CREPSLEY
WRITTEN BETWEEN JANUARY 7TH 2007 AND NOVEMBER 1ST 2011